THE BULLDOGGERS CLUB

THE TALE OF THE
TAINTED BUFFALO WALLOW

THE BULLDOGGERS CLUB SERIES
BOOK 2

BARBARA HAY

THE ROADRUNNER PRESS
OKLAHOMA CITY

Published by The RoadRunner Press
Oklahoma City
www.TheRoadRunnerPress.com

Manufactured by Maple Press, York, Pennsylvania

Library of Congress Control Number: 2013950405

Publisher's Cataloging-In-Publication Data
(Prepared by The Donohue Group, Inc.)

Hay, Barbara.
The Bulldoggers Club. The tale of the tainted buffalo wallow / Barbara Hay. — 1st
ed.

p. : ill. ; cm. — (The Bulldoggers Club series ; bk.2)

Summary: As Opie becomes the newest member of the Club, he joins the Bulldoggers on their first big road trip together. Everything is going according to plan until
they enter the Oklahoma Panhandle and get stranded after a flash flood.
Interest grade level: 4-8.
ISBN: 978-1-937054-57-1 (hardcover)

1. Boys—Societies and clubs—Juvenile fiction. 2. Memory—Juvenile fiction.
3. Voyages and travels—Juvenile fiction. 4. Resourcefulness—Juvenile fiction. 5.
Boys—Fiction. 6. Clubs—Fiction. 7. Memory—Fiction. 8. Voyages and travels—
Fiction. 9. Resourcefulness—Fiction. 10. High interest-low vocabulary books. I.
Title. II. Title: Tale of the tainted buffalo wallow

PZ7.H31382 Tat 2013
[Fic]   2013950405

10 9 8 7 6 5 4 3 2 1

For the victims and families
of the May 2013 Oklahoma tornadoes

"A man only learns by two things,
one is reading, and the other
is association with smarter people."
— Will Rogers,
Oklahoma cowboy
philosopher
(1879 - 1935)

THE BULLDOGGERS CLUB

The Tale of the
Tainted Buffalo Wallow

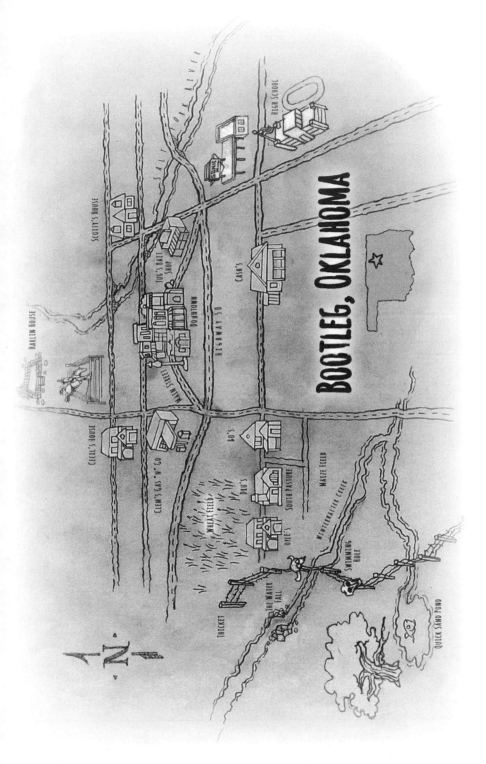

The State of
Oklahoma

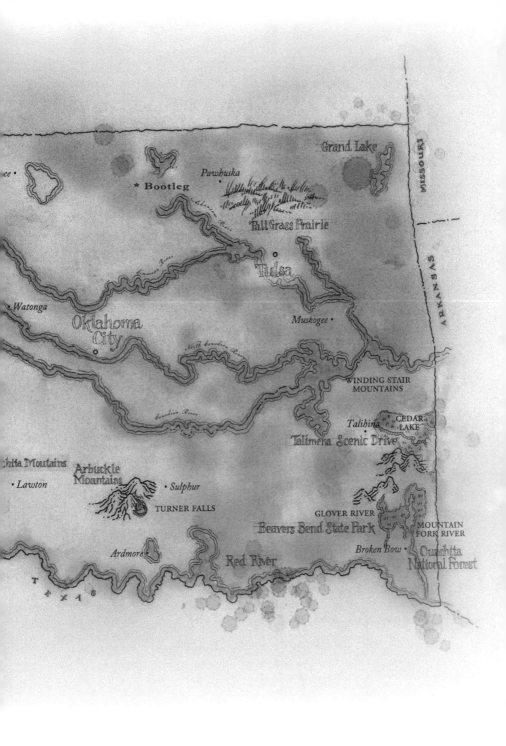

Chapter 1
One Fork's as Good as Another,
Unless It's in the Middle of the Road

AUGUST DAYS IN Oklahoma start out hot and get hotter. We rode along, windows wide open. It hadn't started out that way, but lunch had been foot-long hot dogs with onions and baked beans. Needless to say with six of us—four Bulldoggers and two grown men—squeezed into the extended cab of the truck, the air in Mr. Fender's pickup got dense pretty quick.

The heat just made it worse.

Before we had even pulled back on the highway, Randall (that's how I usually thought of Mr. Fender) had decreed that if anyone had to pass gas he was to gap a window. It didn't take long for the windows to be rolled down, all four of them.

We were pulling a trailer full of livestock from his brother's ranch near Black Mesa, in the far northwestern corner of the Oklahoma Panhandle, where the Rocky Mountains meet the shortgrass prairie.

My horse, Checkers, a bay, and Opie's horse, Moonshine, a gray Standardbred, were riding in the trailer, too. The sixteen calves were destined for the junior rodeo Saturday in Pueblo, Colorado.

We had already crossed more than a couple of cattle guards. By this point, I could have thrown a rock and hit Colorado, I bet. I darn sure could see it. Few places are as flat as the Oklahoma Panhandle. We were still on Fender property—Randall and his brothers own this spread and one back in Bootleg—but it'd been a spell since we'd said our good-byes to more Fenders than I could count. (The only Fender who'd seemed to have been missing was Randall's son Scotty, a fellow Bulldogger, who we'd left back home in Bootleg nursing an injury.)

By this point, bellies still full and plumb worn out from chasing calves, we were riding along half asleep. There was me, Dru. And Bo, my best buddy born two hours before me (something he never lets me forget), and two new members of the Bulldoggers Club, Cash and Opie.

One minute we were hauling that long aluminum cattle trailer, a twenty-eight-footer, blowing white gravel dust behind us in a thick cloud down a country road. The next, we were flying through the air, our mouths open but no sound coming out.

We landed hard. The impact knocked heads together and slammed bodies forward against seat belts. Air bags came at us from every direction. I could tell we were no longer on the road—or at least the truck wasn't. It had skidded over the edge of what had once been a road but was now a landing strip into a gaping ditch below.

We had stopped so sudden-like, the trailer had jumped its hitch and careened sideways. It had stopped at a cockeyed angle just short of the end of the road, its front end protruding over the deep gully.

I heard a moan beside me.

But worse, I heard nothing from the front seat.

We had come on this trip hoping for a little adventure and excitement. I feared we were now talking something more extreme. We were talking life and death.

Chapter 2
Road Trip

IF ANYONE HAD told me when we were planning this road trip that we would never make it to the junior rodeo in Pueblo, Colorado, I might have punched him in the nose for merely suggesting such a thing and gladly accepted the punishment my parents were sure to have doled out.

I remember how excited we were when Randall, Scotty's dad, asked us to go along to help run the calves. We even called an emergency meeting of the Bulldoggers Club to plan the trip. We held the meeting in our new clubhouse—the hayloft in my barn.

Randall had said that we would be responsible for getting the calves ready to go into the chute before they were released during the calf-roping event at the Pueblo rodeo.

Scotty's dad would be the one doing the actual releasing because that has to be done just right. And everyone knew Randall was one of the best at both reading and giving the signals, a nod of the head, when it was time for the calf to be released. Timing is everything in rodeos.

We had never been asked to help run calves before, and we were all feeling the excitement and the pressure of working such a big event. And then, of course, there was the thrill of getting out of town.

Being ranchers, we don't often get to leave the ranch. Someone always has to be there to look after the animals. Each of us has chores we do every morning and every evening—feeding the horses and the cattle, making sure they have fresh water to drink.

We were meeting in the hayloft of my barn because our last clubhouse, an old fraidy hole, had flooded in a big thunderstorm. Once everyone had climbed the ladder into the hayloft and gotten comfortable, I called the meeting to order. Since I don't own a gavel I used a hammer and a small block of wood left from when we replaced the broken step by the back door to my house.

"As president of the Bulldoggers Club, I hereby call this emergency meeting to order," I said, with a pound of my hammer on the wood. "Cecil, as secretary, would you like to call the roll?"

"Sure thing, Dru," Cecil said. "Dru Winterhalter!"

"Here!" I said.

"Bo Gillock!"

"Here!" Bo said.

"Scotty Fender!"

"Here!" Scotty said.

If you count Cecil Rill, who I'm pretty sure knew he was present without calling his own name, that just about took care of the original four Bulldoggers who formed the club. We started the club because we like horses and rodeo and we wanted to prove we were serious about both. Who knew we would end up sharing all kinds of adventures, including catching a state record catfish. Cash Bennett had joined the club after our catfish adventure, and Opie came aboard after moving in near me and Bo. It had seemed the neighborly thing to do; truth be told, it's a rare day when Bootleg sees a newcomer move in, much less one our own age.

"Cash Bennett!" Cecil said.

No answer.

"Cash Bennett!" Cecil hollered looking about the hayloft.

"Huh? Oh, sorry—hey, Dru, did you know you have a litter of kittens up here?"

"Yes, Cash, now could you pay attention. We have a lot to do and not much time to do it in."

"Here," Cash said sheepishly.

"Opie George!"

"He's here, Cecil," I said, getting impatient. "Now could we get to the business at hand? We need to know who will be going on the road trip."

I glanced around at each of the five other members of the Bulldoggers Club.

Scotty lifted his arm, still in a cast. "My mom said no way I can go with a broken wrist. She's right. I wouldn't be much use to you this way."

"I can't go either," Cecil said. "My dad is working a turn-around at the oil refinery, and Grandma needs my help with the chores."

"Okay," I said. "I'm sorry you two aren't able to go with us, but I think we all understand why. That leaves me and Bo . . . you're going, right?"

Bo nodded. "Yep. My dad, too."

"Really?" I said. (Zane Gillock was a former pro rodeo

6

star whose grandfather had worked alongside the African-American-Cherokee rodeo legend Bill Pickett, the man who invented bulldogging, or steer wrestling as it is now known, at the famed 101 Ranch Wild West Show. Mr. Gillock was just about the closest thing we had to a celebrity in Bootleg.)

"Yep. He's been helping out at the Fender place. Scotty's dad has been waiting until my dad felt good enough to go back to work to ask him."

Scotty piped up. "Dad's been trying to hire him on for a long time, but your dad was earning such good money bull ridig that he didn't want to give it up."

"Until he got tossed off that bull, last year," Bo said.

"Ouch!" Cash said.

"You said it," Bo said with a grimace. "Dad was bandaged up like a mummy for weeks after that bull shook him off."

"But now he's back to his old hard-working self," I said.

"That's what I want to do," Cecil said.

"What? Get tossed off a bull or be bandaged like a mummy?" Scotty asked.

"Naw, neither one of those," Cecil said. "I want to steer wrestle on the rodeo circuit. My dad says I have the arm for roping and the grit for wrestling them down."

"We're too young to do that," Opie said, shoving his glasses back up onto his nose.

"No kidding, pip-squeak," Cecil said. "But my dad says in a couple of years, once I've grown a few inches and I've put on some bulk, he's going to start working with me on his days off. He's keeping an eye out for a new horse for me."

"A new horse, that's cool," I said. "What are you going to do with Rocket?"

"Why? You want to buy him from me?"

7

"Uhhh, I dunno. Just curious."

"Haven't decided yet," Cecil said, "but I'll give you first dibs if I do decide to sell him."

"Thanks," I said. "Now back to the trip. So, it'll be me, Bo, Bo's dad, and Scotty's dad."

I nodded at Bo and Scotty; they nodded back. I turned to Cash and Opie, who each occupied a hay bale. "What about you two?"

Opie removed the piece of straw he'd been chewing. "My dad said I could go."

"Me, too," Cash added, but I could tell the kittens still held most of his attention.

"Well, okay," I said. "That should give us enough Bull-doggers to get the job done."

I noticed Cash was now waving his arm like a madman.

"Cash, do you have something to say?" I asked.

"Can we talk about what in the heck we're going to do for ten hours stuck in the backseat of Randall's truck."

"Personally," Bo said, "I plan to catch up on my sleep."

Bo and I exchanged a look. "If I remember Bo, the last field trip we went on," I said, "you were asleep before the bus left the school parking lot."

"What can I say, I need my beauty sleep," Bo said.

The other guys hooted and hollered at that. Cash couldn't resist making some kissing noises. Before things could careen any further off topic, I hammered the meeting back to order.

"Does anyone have a useful answer to Cash's question?" I asked.

"I could bring my Magic cards," Opie said. "If anyone else has some, we could trade."

"That sounds good," Cash said.

"I always take my harmonica on car rides, too," Opie

said. "I can play a whole slew of songs. My dad used to sing along with me till my mom died. Now he just listens."

There was an awkward pause after that, which, to his credit, Opie didn't seem to notice.

"Actually," Bo said, breaking the silence, "that harmonica of yours might come in handy. That's how cowboys on cattle drives used to calm the herd at night. They called it the ole 'tin sandwich.'"

"You should know," I said, "you old history buff."

"I'd like to learn how to play the harmonica," Cecil said.

"I'd be happy to show you sometime," Opie said.

"Okay, now," I said, "back to the business at hand. We're going to need food. It's a long ways to Pueblo."

"My mom always packs a cooler to take," Scotty said. "Dad wouldn't leave home without it."

"I've been on those trips," Cecil said. "She goes a little heavy on the fruits and nuts."

"Borrrring," Cash yodeled.

"Fruits and nuts! I have to agree with Cash on this one," said Bo. "What's a road trip without snacks—and I mean the sweet, salty, no-good-for-you snacks."

Cecil and Bo burst out laughing and fist-bumped.

"Don't you guys worry," Scotty said, "I already talked to Mom. She promised to include some junk food, too."

"Okay, okay," I said, hammering the loft back into order. (My hammer gets quite the workout at even regular meetings of the Bulldoggers; emergency sessions like this have been known to leave my arm in cramps.) "Bo, you be responsible for bringing your own no-good-for-yous. Scotty, we're grateful for whatever your mom would like to send with us, and I know Randall and Zane will be, too."

I heaved a big sigh. "Now, the plan is for us to meet at

my house at five a.m.," I said. "Since we're taking Checkers and Moonshine, and we all live sort of close together on this side of town, Randall said he'll drive over here. He wants to load up and leave by six. He says it is about seven hours west to Kenton, and the ranch where we'll pick up the calves is on the very tip of the Oklahoma Panhandle, almost to New Mexico."

"My Uncle Colton runs that ranch," Scotty said. "He's already worked a bunch of calves so they'll be ready for the junior rodeo kids."

"What do you mean, 'ready'?" Cash asked.

"They take the calves," Scotty explained, "and run them through the chute as if they were in a rodeo event. Uncle Colton and his ranch hand, with some help from local kids who want to practice roping skills, work the calves as if they were competing for real. The calves get used to the routine. They learn to lay still once they are tied up and to run to the other end of the arena afterward."

"It makes it all run smoother," I said. "And you don't waste time chasing calves around the ring after each person has his go."

Cash nodded. "Makes sense."

"Any more questions?" I asked.

They shook their heads, no.

"Okay then, we'll see you bright and early Friday morning," I said.

Bo coughed and gave me a little nod, just like we'd seen Randall do a million times when signaling a cowboy to release a calf.

"Mr. Vice President, do you have something to say?"

"Yes, I do Mr. President. Listen fellows, I know you are excited about our first road trip as a club, but remember, running calves is a hard job. We'll be on our feet from dawn to dusk. And I can tell you from watching my dad and Scotty's, things at a rodeo can go south quickly, whether you're working or competing.

"Everyone needs to get some sleep tonight. And tomorrow, you need to bring your A-game."

"I'm used to working hard," Cash said.

"Me, too," Opie said.

"Sounds just like another day at the ranch to me," I said.

Little did we know how rough it was going to be.

Chapter 3
On the Road

THAT NIGHT I couldn't sleep. I kept waking up. I'd peek under one eyelid at the window, searching for that first ray of daylight, close it tight again, wanting sleep so badly but afraid I would oversleep and be late.

After three or four cycles of this, I gave up and got up. My packed duffle bag for the trip sat at the foot of my bed, along with a rolled-up sleeping bag and pillow. Still in my pajamas, I tiptoed out the door, into the hallway, careful to avoid the squeaky floorboard in front of my three-year-old brother's room.

In the kitchen, the clock on the stove read 3:45. I stared out the window at the barn light. Dad always left that one burning for safety reasons. Now it beckoned to me, as if, during the night, I had been transformed into a June bug.

I grabbed two shiny red apples from the bowl on the table and put one in each pocket. I found my boots by the back door, pulled them on, and quietly slipped out of the house. The warm air on my cheeks was a shock after the coolness of the air-conditioned house.

Checkers must have heard me coming. He whinnied softly, as though he, too, did not want to wake the household. I had put him in his stall before going to bed so I could get him ready this morning in plenty of time for our big adventure. He poked his head over the stall door and watched as I headed straight for the big barrel of oats, my horse's favorite breakfast.

"Hey, bud," I said, opening the door to his stall.

He nuzzled my cheek with his soft brown nose. I poured the oats into his feed bucket. Instead of sticking his nose right in the bucket as he would normally do, he waited.

"You never miss a trick do you," I said, reaching for one of the apples.

As I stroked his neck, I held the apple up for him. He gave me a horsey smile before taking a big bite. Juice ran down my hand. I took a bite from the other side, and we both munched away.

"We have a big adventure ahead of us, Checkers," I said. "Bo and I, being the oldest of the Bulldoggers on this trip, well it is going to fall to us to keep the younger guys on point and safe at the rodeo. I don't want to let Zane and Randall down. It's a lot of pressure on a guy."

Checkers craned his head up and down. I knew he just wanted another bite of apple, but it looked, I swear, like he was nodding in agreement with me.

It was confession time.

"I hardly slept a wink last night, fella, worrying how things will go up there in Pueblo."

Checkers munched, thoughtfully.

13

"I've never been five hundred miles away from Mom and Dad before, and I'm a little nervous," I confided, "but I'll have you there, won't I."

I gave Checkers the rest of the apple, and pulled the last one out of my pocket. I bit into it; the apple was just as juicy and sweet as the first.

"I'm glad we had this little talk, Checkers. I feel better already."

I took one last bite, and then fed the rest of the apple to Checkers. "I best be getting ready to go." I gave him one more good pat and started back to the house.

In the kitchen, my mother was cooking bacon. "Morning," she said, with her back to me.

"How did you know it was me?" I asked.

"Your boots were missing from the mat," she said, as she laid the strips of bacon in a tidy row in the pan.

"That smells good," I said.

"Breakfast won't be long."

"I'm going to miss you, Mom," I said.

"I'm going to miss you, too," she said.

I planted a kiss on her cheek. She smelled of lavender and peppermint.

"You better hurry along, now, honey," she said, shooing me away. But she was smiling that tender smile she saved for special moments like this one.

"Yes, ma'am," I said. "I only have to slip on my clothes. Everything else is done."

"Don't forget, you promised your father that you would turn on the soaker hose along that row of cantaloupes."

"Oh yeah," I said. "I will."

I ran back to my room to dress and grab my gear. I clipped my Swiss Army knife onto the pocket of my jeans. I unzipped my duffle bag and checked through my stuff one more time: A deck of playing cards, two pairs of jeans, two plaid shirts, two white T-shirts, and two pairs of underwear. I searched for socks—check. A plastic zippered bag held a toothbrush, toothpaste, a bar of soap in a plastic box, and a small clear plastic container of shampoo. Next to that, a towel and wash cloth.

Topping it all off: A sketch pad and pencil, to ward off boredom. And, of course, my two favorite magazines, *The Fisherman* and *Outdoor Sportsmen.*

I heard the shuffle of feet behind me, but before I had a chance to turn around, someone clamped his hands over my eyes.

"Guess who?" a deep voice said.

"Zane, is that you?" I asked.

"Nope."

"Kevin?"

Do I sound like your baby brother?"

"Is it my best bud in the whole world?"

"Maybe."

"Maybe nothing!" I pulled the fingers away from my eyes and turned. "I knew it was you!"

"Are you ready?" Bo asked.

"Yep." I zipped my duffle bag and slung it over my shoulder. Bo picked up my sleeping bag and pillow and off we went.

In the kitchen, my mother had plates with eggs, bacon, fried potatoes, and homemade blueberry muffins set out for four. With their usual uncanny timing, Cash and Opie appeared at the back door window. Before they could knock, I had opened the door and ushered them inside. The food disappeared. My mother stood, hands on hips, shaking her head back and forth as we gobbled up in minutes what had taken her an hour to make.

Kevin, came into the kitchen, dragging his blanky, rubbing his sleepy eyes. Before he could make a peep, I heard gravel popping on the drive outside, a sign that Randall had arrived. I whisked Kevin up high in the air, gave him a squeeze, and set him back down. It was time to go.

Outside Randall had parked his new white dually pickup—so called because it has two sets of wheels on the back on each side of the truck—and aluminum stock trailer.

Randall was talking to my father as we drew near.

"You boys ready?" Randall asked.

Zane stepped out of the barn before we could answer.

"No time for lollygagging, Dru," he said. "You boys get your gear loaded right now."

"Yes, sir," I said.

Bo and I exchanged a look. Cash and Opie made short work of putting their gear into the truck bed. After I pitched mine in, I headed to the barn to start loading the tack.

"Need some help?" Bo asked.

I nodded.

Once we were out of earshot, I said, "Your dad was kind of gruff, back there."

"Don't take it personally," Bo said. "They're calling for severe weather where we're headed this weekend. That's enough to put him on edge any day, but whenever he's getting ready to haul this much live flesh, he gets grouchy. After all, when you include the six of us and all of our gear and the stock, we're talking somewhere around fourteen, maybe fifteen thousand pounds. And those critters don't sit in the trailer nice and still like washing machines, either."

"So, basically, your dad is a worrywart." I said as I hefted the saddle and saddle blanket off the rack. Bo grabbed the rope can, bridle, reins, and brush box.

"He is that," Bo said.

We strode out to the trailer. Zane pointed to where to put the tack.

"Has Checkers been fed?" Zane barked.

"Yes, sir," I said.

"Let's get him loaded first then, and then Moonshine."

"Yes, sir," I said.

Opie untied Moonshine's lead rope from the hitching post.

I headed back to the barn. Checkers' head appeared above the stall door, ears perked. I opened the stall door and slipped the halter up Checkers' face and over his ears. I worked it into place, and then hooked a lead rope to it and led him out to the trailer.

By this time, Opie had Moonshine ready, too. We loaded the two horses into the trailer and tied them in.

"Why aren't you putting the horses at the front of the trailer?" Cash asked.

"Because their weight will help to stabilize those back wheels on the highway," Randall said. "They probably weigh, between the two of them, twenty-five hundred pounds."

"Wow! That's more than a Volkswagen Beetle!" Cash looked impressed.

"That placement will also give the tires better traction," Randall added.

"Opie, do you need help loading your tack for Moonshine?" I asked.

With a quick jerk of his head, Opie flung a curtain of blond bangs out of his eyes. "That'd be great," he said.

"Cash why don't you help us get Opie loaded up?" I said.

"Do I have to? I was trying to organize my Magic cards."

"No, you don't have to, but the quicker we get him loaded, the quicker we can leave."

"Oh all right," Cash said, but he seemed none too pleased about it. He shoved the deck of cards into his duffle.

Opie's dad had now arrived, so we went to his truck to unload the rest of the tack.

"Morning, Mr. George," I said.

"Morning, boys," he said, with a swipe of his blond bangs. "Excited about your road trip?"

"You bet," I said.

Opie retrieved the saddle and blanket and lugged them over to the truck's storage compartment at the front of the trailer. I handed Cash the rest.

Mr. George joined us by the trailer. *He looks a little grim*, I thought, and then I overhead him say something that puzzled me: "Opie, don't be afraid to ask for help if you need it."

"Okay, Dad," Opie said, but he didn't sound like he meant it.

"I'm serious," Mr. George said. "You agreed."

"I know," Opie said in a loud whisper. "Shhh, I'll be fine."

Randall and my dad saw Mr. George, and came over to say hello.

"Randall, I don't think you've met Opie's father, T.L. George."

The two men shook hands.

"Pleasure," Randall said.

"T.L. moved up here to Oklahoma State University from Baylor, a couple of months ago."

"Thomas, here," Randall nodded at my dad, "has told me lots of good things about you and Opie. I was very sorry to hear about your wife."

"I appreciate that, and thank you for inviting Opie along this weekend. Here I was worried about him making new friends, and he's already gotten himself invited on a road trip. He's doing better at meeting new people than his old man."

With a nod at the truck, he said, "That's a mighty fine rig you have there, Randall. I wondered how you were going to fit all the boys in, but that extended cab looks like it will do the job."

"I've been threatening to buy a new rig for years, but never could bring myself to do it," Randall said. "Finally, I broke down . . . the old trailer I was using had nothing left to give. A couple of weeks ago, I got to thinking about this road trip and realized the time had come."

Randall led Opie's dad around the truck and trailer, pointing out the various features, as if he were a car salesman himself. When he started rambling on about cross members and the uncoupling trailer latch, he lost me.

Tour finished, Randall said, "We best be loading up."

On cue my mother came out of the house with Kevin in tow. I hurried over to give them both one last hug. My dad, too. When I turned back, Mr. George had his hand on Opie's shoulder, giving him what must have been some pretty serious last minute instructions, because Opie was frowning and nodding. Finally, Mr. George gave Opie a long hug.

We were just about to load up when Scotty, with his broken arm, and his mother, Arlene, drove up. They hopped out of their old pickup and made a beeline for Randall. They exchanged words and he followed them back to their truck, where he pulled a large cooler from the bed. I could only imagine what Mrs. Fender must have packed inside that hefty-looking chest.

"It's six o'clock, boys," Randall hollered. "Time to get on the road."

We let Cash and Opie climb into the second seat first so Bo and I could sit next to each other. Cash had no more settled in than he glanced around and frowned: "Where's the DVD player?"

"Doesn't appear to have one," I said.

"What are we going to do all day if there's no player?"

"I brought some things," Opie said.

"We could play a road-trip game," Bo suggested.

"That's just lame," Cash said.

"Have you ever played any?" Bo asked.

"Well, no," Cash said.

"It'll be fun," I said. "Man, I can't wait to see Colorado. I've never been, but I looked up pictures on the Internet of the Rocky Mountains."

"Yeah," Bo said, "I can't wait to see Pikes Peak."

"Me, either," Opie said.

Randall and Zane climbed into the front seat. As we pulled away, the last thing I saw was Kevin, the thumb of one hand jammed into his mouth, waving like crazy with the other hand.

Chapter 4
No Man's Land

W E DROVE RIGHT THROUGH the center of town, but it was too early for most folks to be out of their beds, much less out and about. I think Randall and Zane would have preferred to have us Bulldoggers go back to sleep, too, now that we were on the road, but we were way too excited.

"Mr. Fender, how far is it to Pueblo?" I asked.

"And so it starts," Zane said, with a laugh. "Wonder how many times we're going to hear that question before we reach the rodeo grounds?"

Randall chuckled. "It's normally about a thirteen-hour drive, Dru," Randall said, "but we're hauling a lot of cargo so it could take us eight or nine just to get to my brother's ranch outside Kenton."

"That's in the Panhandle," Bo said.

"Yep, what they used to call 'No Man's Land,'" Randall

said. "It has always been a wild and dangerous place. And it still can be today. In winter, blizzards howl down from the Arctic, freezing men and animals. In the summer, dust storms steamroll across the high plains. And come spring and late summer there are tornadoes that can uproot trees and hurl cattle and houses through the air.

"That said, today is a cakewalk compared to the 1800s. After the Civil War, it was mostly cattlemen who dared brave it—and even then only to drive the herds north from Texas into Kansas for shipment to market. The 1862 passage of the Homestead Act opened No Man's Land to settlement, though I don't think Uncle Sam really expected anyone to come. But come they did—'nesters,' hardworking folks trying to find their own little piece of land and the American dream. Unfortunately the nesters were followed by outlaws and con men eager to exploit the area's lack of order.

"You see there was no law there then," Randall said.

"What do you mean 'there was no law'?" I said.

Opie piped up, "There were no sheriffs or judges to hold people accountable."

"Is that true?" I looked at Randall.

"Yes, sir. Opie's right."

"Of course he is," I muttered under my breath. "So, what did folks do when those bad guys came around, Mr. Fender?"

Opie started to answer but I held up my hand and gave him a warning eye, "I was asking him."

"It sometimes wasn't pretty," Randall said, "I heard tell about one unlucky cuss who was overheard bragging about rustling some cattle. Before he had a chance to even take the animals, folks came along and took matters into their own hands. Hung him from a nearby tree.

"And then there's the story of the Man with Two Names. They say his spirit still haunts the spot where the town of Mesa used to be, but then Mesa itself is only a memory now."

Something on the highway distracted Randall then, but Opie jumped in.

"What Mr. Fender didn't say is that hangings were so common in those days, people had a thesaurus of words and ways to say it. Some were active descriptions—'use him to trim a tree' is one of my favorites, while others were more visual—'midair dance' or 'strangulation jig.' Some made it sound like a party: 'necktie social' or 'Texas Cakewalk.'"

I had heard enough. "Stop! I'm going to hang you up by your hide if you don't change the subject."

Opie took one look at my face and stopped talking.

I didn't have the guts to tell him I was pretty sure his hanging trivia was going to give me nightmares for the next week. My neck had already started to itch.

Chapter 5
Lame Games People Play

CASH WASTED NO time in calling Bo on his offer. He turned sideways in his seat to face Bo and me. "What about that road-trip game?"

"Banana," Bo said.

"Banana who?" Cash said, and laughed out loud.

"It's not a knock-knock joke," Bo said, laughing in spite of himself. "When you see a yellow vehicle . . ."

"It used to be a yellow VW beetle," I said.

"A what?" Cash said.

"You know, a Volkswagen bug," I said.

"We changed it," Bo said, "because Beetles got too few and far between."

"Yeah," I said, "so we changed it to any yellow vehicle."

"When you see one, you yell out 'banana,'" Bo said. "You win if you see the most. Now, if you do happen to see a VW bug, of any color, you holler 'slug bug, no tag backs,' and punch someone in the arm."

"Anyone?" Cash asked, like it was some kind of trick.

"Yep, *anyone*," I said.

Randall countered from the driver's seat. "Woah, wait a minute boys. Zane and I are off limits, and I don't much like the idea of you punching each other either, especially with us being on the highway. Why don't you . . . uh . . . touch fists?"

"Fist bump?" I said.

"Yeah, that. Just do that," Randall said.

"Okay," we all said at once.

The eastern sun threw a slight glow above the horizon behind us. We were headed west. I could see it rising in the large side mirror on my side of the truck. Ahead of us, it was still pitch dark. The beams of the headlights shining like ray guns on the blacktop.

"Haven't seen another truck for a while . . . or a car, for that matter," Cash said.

"Me, either," Opie said.

"The only other thing moving aside from us was that tumbleweed a ways back. I thought it was a ghost, flying up over the hood like that," I said.

"It scared the bejeebers out of me," Bo said.

"It's going to be hard to see much of anything until the sun comes up," Zane said. "Now might be a good time to catch up on some sleep."

As much as we tried, not one of us could fall asleep, not even Bo, despite his super human ability to normally fall asleep anywhere, anytime. *Guess there are exceptions to everything,* I thought.

Before too long, though, the sun was up and along with it came more traffic. As the hours passed, the traffic was reduced to a smattering of cars and trucks in the small cross-road towns. Vehicles the color of bananas proved scarce.

One of the only two we saw was an old school bus parked in someone's back pasture; it had faded to the shade of watered-down lemonade, I'm not proud to say the bus was my call.

"I told you this game was lame," Cash said, when the bus was ruled eligible by Bo and Opie. If I had had a muzzle right then, I'd have been tempted to see if it fit Cash.

We made a pit stop in Alva, and I dug out my magazines from my duffle bag so I'd have something to distract me from Cash's whining on the next leg of the trip. I offered my sketch pad and pencils to Opie, but Opie had brought his own, so Cash took them. Bo and I shared the magazines. I tried not to resent Cash using up the little art paper I had left; I told myself it was like how Mom distracts Kevin with her purse when he won't settle down on Sunday drives.

You learn things about people on a long road trip. I now realized Opie was something akin to a living, breathing encyclopedia. I had been listening to him recite the ways the word "cutting" is used by cowboys for at least fifty miles. It had started with a simple disagreement about what makes a good cutting horse, what makes one horse good at singling out and isolating calves from the herd. We all had opinions. But who knew Opie had so many thoughts on just the word!

". . . and then there is 'cut 'er loose' and 'cutting the herd,'" he said, "but I bet you never heard of 'cut a big gut.'" He took a breath.

"You sure you didn't make that last one up?" I asked.

"Nope. I read it in a book."

He dozed off then. I was beginning to realize the only time Opie was quiet was when he was sleeping or eating.

Luckily our next stop was lunch at a roadside picnic area outside of Guymon. Randall and Zane made a fire in the grill, while we Bulldoggers made sure the horses had water. We tossed a football around Randall had brought until lunch was ready.

I couldn't remember the last time a hot dog and baked beans had tasted so good, and said so.

"Everything tastes better on a road trip," Bo observed.

We reached Kenton and the Fender ranch a couple of hours later. With Zane keeping one eye on the clock and one eye on the sky, we loaded the stock at record speed.

As we left the ranch, the blue flat-topped mesas and high plateau told us we were not only near the highest point in Oklahoma—Black Mesa at 4,973 feet—but also already in the foothills of the Rocky Mountains. We could still see for miles in most every direction, but we didn't need any tumbleweeds to tell us it was cowboy country.

So far the trip has gone pretty much as planned, I thought. *Fun, but no surprises.*

Chapter 6
Spills and Accidents Happen

CRASH! THUD! One minute we were air borne in the truck; the next, we had landed. Hard. The impact triggered screams and cries both human and animal. It was terrifying. I had never been in a car wreck before but I didn't think it was something one ever got comfortable with.

Once the screaming quieted and the dust settled, we all looked to Randall and Zane to tell us what to do: Get out of the truck. Stay in the truck. Move. Don't move. But they didn't respond. They both appeared to be asleep in the front seat, and then we realized, all of us at once, that was not the case.

We unsnapped our seat belts and slid forward to see if they were dead or alive. The truck's weight shifted with the movement, lurching forward, sliding deeper into the gully. The calves, poor things, were piled up in the trailer, mewling panicked cries for help. We could now see that Randall, who had been driving, was slumped over, unconscious—or dead. Bo's dad, Zane, had blood running down his face.

Before we could do think or move, Zane roused. I saw him wipe a hand over his face. He stared at the hand, now covered in blood, as though he could not figure out where the blood had come from. I have never seen him as stunned, even when that rodeo bull threw him off and he landed so hard in the dirt. It took months for him to recover from that fall. He still walks with a limp.

Bo had been thrown closer to Randall's side of the truck. He called out his name, trying to wake him. No response. He scrambled closer and shook his arm. Randall moaned and slowly stirred.

"Are you all right?" Bo's fear put an edge on his voice.

Randall's eyes popped open.

"What happened?" He took in the whole cockeyed scene in one look: The truck's nose halfway in the ditch, the jack-knifed trailer, and the restless sounds of animals inside kicking and stomping in their confusion.

Randall turned and saw Zane gazing back at him, wild-eyed. I could tell he was as concerned about Zane as I was by the deep crease that had appeared between his bushy eyebrows. Randall caught me staring at Zane.

"Are you boys all okay?" he croaked. When he turned slightly in his seat, I noticed him wince as if in pain.

"What's wrong?" I asked.

"Not sure," Randall said. "My ankle seems to have taken the brunt of the hit, but that's the least of our worries. If you and the other boys are okay, we need to check the livestock . . . and you boys are going to have to do it, I think, because Zane is going into shock. We need to get him out of this vehicle, but slowly and carefully. We don't want to upset the apple cart."

I pushed open my passenger door and peered into the rocky, dusty ditch below, what had just seconds before been a flat road . . . a good ten feet higher in elevation. I reached back into the cab for my cowboy hat, put it on, and stepped down onto the running board. I walked the length of it, holding onto the side, back to the bed of the truck, and climbed inside. I felt the truck edge forward. I froze in place. The driver's side door opened. Randall peered out, frowning as if anticipating the hurt he was in for before this was all over.

"Randall, we'll figure out a way to get you down," I said. "Cash, come on out of there."

Cash poked his head out, gazing at the ditch far below.

"Come on," I said, "everyone out, but go easy."

Cash inched his way along the running board and into the truck bed.

"There's a stepladder tied up in the trailer," I said to no one in particular.

"If we can get to it," Bo said. He had followed Cash. Opie had gone out the other passenger door and had made his way around to the truck bed about the same time as Bo.

The livestock trailer was its own challenge. The calves and horses had calmed some when they heard our voices, but that didn't last long. Soon, they were stomping and flailing and bawling, making everyone jittery.

Out of the blue, Opie started singing "Old Man River" in a high-pitched voice, and by George if those critters didn't start listening. It seemed to put everyone at ease.

But every time one of us moved, the pickup creaked and moved a smidgen or two in the wrong direction. It seemed determined to slip off the edge, and it made me want to hurry us on out of there. If the truck went over it could possibly flip, so it was urgent that we find a way to hold it steady until we could get Randall and Zane to safety.

Bo must have been thinking the same thing because he said, "There's an old dead tree trunk over here. We could tie the axle to it with one of our catch ropes."

I nodded, "I see a fence post that might do the trick, too."

I opened the rope can and grabbed a catch rope for both of us, handing one to Bo. We eased ourselves out of the truck and down to the ground, careful not to move too suddenly. Bo tied one end of his rope to the axle and looped the lasso end over the tree trunk. I tied mine to the axle and looped the fence post.

Cash and Opie had eased themselves down to the ground by the time we finished securing the truck.

"Not sure how long it'll hold, so we better be quick," Bo said. "If we can get that fencing out of the trailer and erected we can corral the calves as they come off." He was talking about the eight-foot portable fence panels we use to make chutes to guide the calves into the corrals at the rodeo. Cash and Opie nodded, indicating they were ready to help.

"That ladder is all the way to the front of the trailer," I said. "It might be quicker to use Checkers, than trying to wade through the stock."

Bo scratched his head, thinking. "If he'll hold still next to that creaky pickup."

"If that doesn't work we'll get the ladder," I said.

Before we could make a move, the pickup inched forward again, pushing more gravel over the edge.

"What if the truck rolls down over the top of you and Checkers, Dru? What'll we do then?" Bo paced in a circle.

"We have the truck steadied for the moment," I said.

"With any luck it'll hold long enough for us to get them out."

"Hey! Where'd you boys get to?" Randall hollered.

"We're right here," I hollered, and Bo and I headed back to the cab.

Randall wore the same frown he gets when he is tired of waiting for us to load up for a trip to town.

"We're trying to figure out how to secure the truck so it will stay put until we can get you both out," Bo said.

"Good job," Randall said. "Zane needs out of the heat of this truck and to a cooler spot."

When we had started out from Bootleg at six a.m. the thermometer in the truck had read eighty-five degrees Fahrenheit. We had stopped for lunch outside of Guymon about noon. I could tell by the angle of the sun now that it was almost mid-afternoon.

The heat was coming off the earth in ripples. The hot Oklahoma sun would turn the inside of the truck into a pizza oven in no time. Thank goodness Zane had insisted we leave early in hopes of avoiding the bad weather rolling in. Nobody wanted to be unloading livestock in the middle of a thunderstorm, much less a tornado like the one they had had over in Cimarron County yesterday.

"Okay, Mr. Fender." Bo's voice quivered.

With that, we got right to work. I unlatched the tailgate on the trailer and, together, Bo and I swung it open. Checkers whinnied nervously. He was not usually so antsy, but from the look in his eyes and the way his ears were pinned back flat against his head, I could tell he was scared. I untied his lead rope from the trailer and talked softly to him as I led him out.

"Come on, boy. Zane needs your help. He's injured, and I'm not sure how bad."

"Bo!" Randall called out. "Grab that neck brace from the emergency medical kit."

Bo hurried round to the front of the trailer and combed the storage compartment for the kit. When he found it, he hauled it over to the ground, flipped open the lid of the metal box, found what he was hunting for, and came back with it.

Being veteran rodeo riders, we always have handy all sorts of braces, splints, and wraps for bum knees and wrists. Sooner or later everyone gets thrown and injured. Nowadays, most bull riders actually wear a neck and back brace while competing to prevent injury.

Leading Checkers, I followed Bo, Cash, and Opie to the edge of the road and peered over into the ditch. I looked at Bo just as Bo turned his head to look at me. The ditch was deeper than we realized.

What do we do now, I wondered?

Chapter 7
Prepare a Place

NONE OF US HAD GIVEN much thought to how we would get Zane onto Checkers' back, once we managed to get down to where he was.

"Someone will have to help Zane out of the truck," I said. "Any volunteers?"

"Maybe Randall could help him out," Bo said.

"I don't think so—if he and Zane both get on that side, all the weight will shift over there, and the truck is already leaning that way," I said.

"Maybe we could get Randall onto Checkers first, and then go around and get Zane," Cash suggested.

"That won't work either," Opie piped up. He adjusted his wire-framed eyeglasses on his nose. "Randall is keeping the weight of the truck balanced. If he gets out first, then Zane's weight could cause the truck to tilt further, sort of like when you're seesawing and one person gets off."

"All I know," Bo said, "is we better quit jawing and do something. Let's ask Randall."

"Good idea," I said.

"Randall," Bo hollered. "We brought Checkers here for you to climb onto, but we're afraid that might throw the truck off balance, so we're not sure what to do."

"You have the neck brace, right?"

"Yes, sir," Bo said.

"The safest thing would be for Dru to ride Checkers around there. Go up the road a piece to where you can access the ditch easier, and then have Dru put the neck brace on Zane. He hit his head hard. I can't tell how badly he's hurt, but it will stabilize his neck somewhat. Then Dru can help him climb onto Checkers. Meanwhile, Bo, you go prepare a place in the shade where your dad can lay down.

"Once Zane is situated, Dru can come back for me. And Cash and Opie, I should have some orange cones in the truck bed—place two behind the trailer to warn oncoming traffic. Then you two get those fence panels up so we can get the animals off that trailer."

"Yes, sir," we all chimed together.

There was no way to get our tack so I led Checkers to a big rock, so I could easily mount him bareback. It's not unusual for me to ride bareback at home. In fact, that is how I first learned to ride. But this was No Man's Land, a place where thieves, cattle rustlers, and murderers once hid to avoid hanging or jail time. I thought about how Randall had said they called it No Man's Land not because no one wanted to live here but because almost no one *could* it was such harsh, unforgiving land.

I tried to remember what else I knew about the area. We had learned in geography that the Panhandle had once been covered by shallow seas. After they evaporated, volcanic gasses pushed up the Rocky Mountains, leaving Oklahoma with an eastward tilt.

The constant flow of the rivers that remained—the Salt Fork of the Arkansas River, and the Cimarron—ate through the rock creating buttes and mesas. Shortgrass prairies fed massive herds of buffalo as the massive animals moved across the Great Plains according to the season.

No sign of those buffalo herds remained except for the buffalo wallows they left behind. No outlaws who once called this place home endured either, but still this was No Man's Land, lonely isolated country . . . no telling who might be hiding out in these parts at this very second.

I shoved my hat down tighter on my head and rode to the rescue.

Chapter 8
Ouch!

I WAS SOAKED WITH sweat, all the way through my jeans and shirt. Flies buzzed and bit us, but at least Checkers had a tail to swish to help keep them at bay. I rode the length of the ditch till I found a place that wasn't so steep, where Checkers could step down, and then we followed the ditch to the truck. Atop Checkers, I was high enough to reach the passenger door handle of the pickup. Zane's window was rolled down. He looked up and saw me and smiled that crooked little smile of his—the result of a run in with a colt when he was a boy. The colt's hoof had split his lip and that's just how it healed.

I opened Zane's door and urged Checkers closer so I could get at Zane. His seat belt held him against the seat, but I knew as soon as the buckle released there was a chance he might not be able to keep from falling out of the truck. I reached up and wrapped the neck brace around his neck.

All the while he stoically stared at me, not participating at all—so unlike the Zane who loved to joke around and always had something to say.

When all was ready, Randall unhooked the seat belt, and I caught Zane as it let him go. He seemed to understand that he was to get on Checkers. With a little help he lifted his right leg enough for me to guide it over the horse's back.

Once he was seated, I wrapped my arms around him and turned Checkers back the way we had come so he could step out easily.

Bo had spread horse blankets on the ground under one of the rare trees to be found, a scraggly blackjack oak. Opie and Cash had managed to put up two of the fence panels, one on each side of the trailer. They met Checkers and me to help Zane off and over to the blankets. Zane moaned loudly as he stretched out in the shade of the tree.

Checkers and I then quickly retraced our steps, back to the pickup, only this time to the driver's side door. Randall's face drew up in a wry grin at the sight of us. He eased opened his door, wincing in pain as he prepared to stand so he could mount Checkers. With his good leg on the running board, he raised his injured leg up and over Checkers. He lowered himself slowly behind me and wrapped his arms around my waist. I grabbed Checkers' mane to turn him away from the truck . . .

Crack!

The old tree trunk, the one we'd tied the truck to so it wouldn't move, had broken in half from the weight.

The truck lurched forward. Gravel spit in all directions.

I grabbed Checkers' mane tighter and gripped his belly tight with my knees, like a vice. Checkers' ears flattened against his head and he sidestepped. When he did, Randall lost his seat—Checkers went one way, Randall went the other. Randall tightened his arms around me as he fell and took me down with him.

He landed hard on his shoulder with me on top of him.

"Owwwww," he screamed in pain.

"Owwwwww," I screamed back from sheer fright. I scrambled to my feet.

Snap!

The air shook, and next thing I knew, the truck tumbled over into the rocky ditch, throwing dust and gravel into the air behind it.

When the truck finally stopped moving and the dust cloud cleared, Randall's brand new truck was resting on its crumpled rooftop. The frayed end of the lasso dangled from the rear axle. The impact had opened the toolbox and flung tools in every direction. Good thing the trailer was no longer hitched to the truck.

Checkers was nowhere to be seen.

Randall was moaning on the ground.

I stood staring up at where just seconds ago the truck had been, stunned.

How will we ever get Randall out now, I wondered.

Chapter 9
Dead Zone

RANDALL WAS IN pain. One look at his tight face said it all. He laid on the ground gingerly cradling his shoulder with his other arm. Cash and Opie and Bo stood on the ragged edge of the road peering down on us. The horrified looks on their dirty, sweaty faces underscored the seriousness of the situation we now found ourselves in.

I whistled for Checkers, not knowing what else to do. *How far had he run?* I took a deep breath and tried to gather my wits about me. Randall moaned and I hurried over to his side. I knelt, unsure what to do next.

He tossed me a sideways glance. "My shoulder is dislocated," he said, between gritted teeth. "You're going to have to help me put it back into place before the muscles start tightening up."

"We should call for help," I said, feeling nauseated. "I'll call 9-1-1."

"Good idea," Randall patted his chest pocket and sighed in relief. "At least I still have my cell phone."

He looked at it and grimaced. "No service. I forgot; it's a dead zone out here."

"A dead zone?"

"No cell phone towers for miles. I can't make any phone calls."

"Maybe Zane's cell phone will work," I said.

"Nope. Nobody's will work. We can't even call 9-1-1."

Now I grimaced.

"The CB radio was in the truck," Randall said, "but no telling where it might be now."

We both glanced over at the truck lying on its roof—the antenna broken off.

"Doesn't matter where the CB is if there's no antenna," Randall said. "We can't get a signal without it."

"So what do we do now?"

I had not worried too much before about us getting out of here—even after the truck flipped—because Randall and Zane always knew what to do, but when I realized that we had no way to call for help, I admit, it felt as if buzzards were waging war in my stomach. Maybe it was hunger pangs but my gut told me it was pure terror.

Several feet from the pickup, the ice chest sat upside down; its contents flung every which way. I'm pretty sure all those bags of ice we had dumped in there, before leaving Guymon, were melting away . . . along with any hope of making it to Pueblo anytime soon.

Chapter 10
Higher Ground

"NOT ENOUGH TIME TO wait for help," Randall said. His breathing was shallow as if it hurt to draw air into his lungs.

"What do you mean?" I asked, afraid of his answer.

"You're going to play doc for me. Don't worry; I'll tell you what to do," he said. "Now get behind me and help me sit up."

Randall was holding his arm up and away from his body. An ugly knot bulged his sleeve in an odd location.

"Are you sure it isn't broken?" I asked, and knelt beside him. I wasn't sure how to go about helping him to sit up without hurting him more.

Before Randall could answer, Bo was beside me and we were lifting Randall into a sitting position.

"I don't know where you came from," I said to Bo, "but I'm glad you are here."

Bo nodded but he looked a little shaky.

Randall directed, "Bo, I need you to take off your shirt, roll it up, and wrap it tight around my chest."

Bo did as instructed.

"Now hold tightly onto both ends, and Dru, while Bo is providing countertraction, you are going to pull my arm at a forty-five- to ninety-degree angle away from my body."

I did not like the sound of that. The fear of causing him more pain made me gulp.

"Even if I holler, Dru," Randall said, seeming to read my mind, "don't stop. You have to do it. It'll be okay, son."

Easier said than done, I thought. *What if I do it wrong? What if I break Scotty's Dad! Scotty would never forgive me. And I'd never forgive myself.* I nodded. *Get a grip. It's never wise to lose your head in an emergency,* I told myself.

Randall seemed to know the sooner I focused on the details, the easier this would go.

"It'll be easier for you, Dru," he instructed, "if you can tie something to my arm and then tie the other end around your body so you can use your weight and keep your hands free to guide my arm back into the socket."

Beads of sweat broke out on my forehead. At the mention of the word socket, bile rose in my throat. I covered my mouth, scrambled away, and vomited in the dirt.

The sound of hoof beats made me turn to look. It was Opie on Moonshine. Opie slid off onto the ground carrying a catch rope and some rags. *I've never been so happy to see the little know-it-all,* I thought.

Opie set right to work wrapping rags around Randall's forearm and wrist. Then he tied the catch rope over that, securing it with a slipknot. He tied one end of the rope around his waist. "Ready, Bo?" Opie asked.

I was still a little stunned—both from our predicament and Opie riding in to save my day. I wiped my mouth with my sleeve, knelt behind Randall, and watched as Opie leaned steadily back on the rope and began maneuvering Randall's arm. I could tell Randall was fighting not to holler, biting his bottom lip hard enough to draw blood, but just about the time Opie had relocated the ball of the arm joint back in the socket, a cry escaped Randall's lips.

He fell limply against me. The brim of his cowboy hat hit my chin solidly. The hat bounced off Randall's sweaty head and rolled into the dirt. His head hung limply on his chest, and I was afraid we had lost him, when just as fast he came to again. He groaned deep in his throat, and then blinked away the confusion. He didn't seem to understand where Opie had come from. He looked over at Bo, who was still holding tightly to the sleeves of his shirt, and his mind appeared to clear.

"Thank you, boys," Randall said, finally.

Bo turned to me and Opie. "How are we going to get him out of this ditch?"

"First, I'm going to splint his ankle," Opie said. He pushed up his wire frames with his thumb, untied first himself and then Randall, and stood. He walked over to Moonshine, pulled the saddlebags he had thrown over his back to the ground, and began rummaging through them until he found what he was after. Then back he came.

"What you got there?" I asked.

"First aid supplies. I always carry them," Opie said. "Now Randall's boot has acted somewhat as a splint, but I'm going to reinforce it with these sticks I found. I'm going to wrap them with Ace bandages to secure them until we can get him moved to higher ground."

Opie set to work and soon had Randall's boot wrapped and ready for him to be moved.

"I think the best way for us to move him will be to make a chair with our arms and carry him," Opie said. "Dru, can you help him to stand?"

I positioned myself by Randall's good arm, leaned down, and put his arm around my neck. I moved slowly and carefully. Randall got his good leg under him so he would be able to stand as I lifted him. Bo and Opie grabbed each other by the forearms and, as I raised Randall from the ground, Bo and Opie slid in behind him with their makeshift arm chair.

It took all four of us, but we got Randall back to the spot where Checkers and I had been able to step down into the ditch—but not without switching places a time or two. Randall was heavier than he looked.

What I didn't understand was how Opie had come to know what he did about first aid. I knew he was a brainiac and spent a lot of time with his nose in a book—maybe he'd been a Boy Scout in a past life—but he acted like someone who had real-life experience to go with all that book learning.

I thought I had detected a slight limp when he walked sometimes, but had just figured it was his poor attempt at a cowboy swagger, you know, like John Wayne's straight-legged walk.

Maybe there's more to him than meets the eye, I thought.

I would not get the chance to ask him, because, at the moment, we had bigger knots to untie.

Chapter 11
Opie's Secret

BY THE TIME we got Randall out of the ditch and over to the tree, Zane, at least, seemed to be feeling better. Cash had stayed with Zane while we were helping Randall, but I could see that the scraggly canopy of the tree was not going to provide enough shade for two full grown men.

I hoped Randall might have a suggestion or two on what we should do first, because when the pickup flipped it had tossed out not only the cooler but also tools, water jugs, and anything else not bolted down. The livestock was still on the trailer, but Checkers was still nowhere to be seen.

Randall, having been in tough situations before, did not seem fazed. He gathered us all around him with a wave of his good arm and a wince.

"Boys, as you can see, we've gotten ourselves into a bit of a fix, but I've been in worse, so don't fret none. There's always a way out and with the six of us working together, we're going to be fine."

Randall drew a slow breath. "First off, since both Zane and I bumped our heads, we will need you boys to wake us up, on the hour, if we happen to doze off. Concussions can play dirty tricks on a fella."

He did not have to tell us about concussions. Being Bulldoggers, we had heard tell about many a cowboy or bull rider who never woke up again after taking a hard knock to the head.

"Yes, sir," we said in unison.

"Second, since we're in a dead zone, I can't call the rodeo organizer in Pueblo." He sighed. "If I'm right, they probably won't notice the missing livestock until tomorrow morning."

Bo and I exchanged glances. Cash kicked the dirt with the toe of his boot. Opie shoved his hands deeper in his pockets.

"That being the case," Randall said, "we better prepare to spend the night out here. It's only going on four o'clock. That gives us plenty of time to set up camp before dark.

"Dru, you and Opie take Moonshine and go scavenge whatever you can from the wreck that used to be my new pickup. I would wager Checkers has settled down and has come wandering back our way by now.

"Bo, you and Cash stay here. Maybe, between us, we can rig up those fence panels into a corral so we can get those animals off the trailer."

"Yes, sir," we chimed.

Opie grabbed Moonshine's mane and slipped a rope on him. I gave Opie a boost onto his back and then Opie offered an arm to help me swing up behind him. With a click of his tongue, Opie nudged Moonshine forward. No one would know it from his slow plodding pace but Moonshine

had once been a pony horse. I don't mean a *race horse*—that's a whole different kind of horse. No, a pony horse is one used to walk the racing horses to the starting gate at a race track.

I glanced back at Bo. He was looking after us with such a drawn face, I thought he might be about to cry. I couldn't blame him. If my dad was injured and hurting the way Zane was, I would be glum, too—and afraid. He caught me looking at him and waved me off, with a tiny smile.

Knowing Bo the way I do, I knew if there was a way to rig shelter for Randall and Zane, he would figure it out—but I also suspected that Cash would be little help, except maybe for standing and holding things in place.

As we rode along, I said, "Thanks for helping back there."

"It was nothing," said Opie.

"It was amazing, is what it was," I said. "How'd you know what to do with his arm?"

"I read a lot."

"Nobody could do that just from reading about it."

"Actually, you'd be surprised," Opie said. "I know of a mother who reroofed her house by herself, simply by reading the how-to instructions in a Time-Life book she kept beside her on the roof. And then there's the man who learned to make an underwater camera by . . ."

I must have looked doubtful, because he stopped short of finishing his sentence.

"It's true, Bulldogger's honor! But in my case you're also right. When I lost my leg, I was lucky enough to have some good people who were well trained and knew what to do. They saved my life, and I vowed to be like them. Besides reading all the books I could, I took a first aid—"

"Wait a minute!" I interrupted. "Go back. What do you mean, lost your leg?"

"Look!" Opie hollered, pointing. "There's Checkers! He's way over there, munching on buffalo grass, behind that mess of junipers."

Opie nudged Moonshine into a trot just as I whistled for Checkers. Checkers paused in his eating long enough to raise his head. I couldn't say if he recognized us.

"I'm happy to see him," I said, as we drew closer. "Not surprised he found buffalo grass. My mom would say he's an emotional eater."

We both laughed. It was a welcome release of tension.

Opie steered Moonshine between the scruffy juniper bushes and up alongside Checkers. I grabbed his mane and slid across onto his back, reaching for his reins. Opie turned back toward the wreck, and, as I followed him on Checkers, I could not help wondering exactly how he had lost his leg, and why it had never occurred to me before to ask him about his limp. I'm guessing I was so focused on the annoying parts of Opie, I never gave a second thought as to how he came to be the way he was. I felt a little ripple of discomfort, or could it be conscience?

"I sure could use a drink," I said.

"Me, too."

Opie had no sooner answered than he reined Moonshine to a stop and peered at the road ahead. "Oh no," he groaned.

I pulled up alongside him and followed his gaze to the pickup.

"I was afraid of that," he said.

"Afraid of what?"

"The water jugs did not survive."

We dismounted. Checkers and Moonshine moseyed over to nibble on a grassy patch nearby. One by one Opie located, lifted, and shook each of the blue, five-gallon plastic wa-

51

ter jugs, scattered across the crash site. "Every darn one of them is empty," he said, as he examined the last jug. "See, it's cracked from the impact. And the ones that aren't cracked were empty to begin with."

"I'm sure some things survived the crash," I said. "Let's spread out and see what else we can find."

Opie nodded. We piled the jugs up, and took off in opposite directions, scanning the ground for anything with possibility.

I found the cooler and its contents covered in dirt and ants. "I had hoped we might be able to salvage something to eat from this," I said, loud enough for Opie to hear me.

Opie shrugged. "If we don't have water, we shouldn't eat anyway because it takes water for digestion. And digestion warms the body, and, in this heat, we don't need to be warmer."

I found nothing encouraging in his words.

Our duffles had been thrown free of the truck and seemed to have survived intact. Before too long, we had assembled a hodgepodge of items, none of which could quench my growing thirst.

"My tongue feels like a giant ball of cotton in my mouth," I said.

"On second thought," Opie said, "we're all going to be useless in this heat, without water. Maybe we should focus our energy on that."

"Hey, I just remembered something," I said.

I ran to the truck cab and peered inside. "Found it." There, on the ceiling-turned-floor was my half full bottle of pop. I reached in, pulled it out, and was about to open it, when Opie stopped me.

"That will only dehydrate you more."

"Are you sure?" The pop, even if it was now warm and flat, was mighty tempting, especially as dry as my throat felt.

"I'm sure," Opie said. "What we need to do is use this heat to make our own water."

"People don't make water," I said. "Rain makes water, ice makes water, snow makes water, but people don't."

"Yes they can," Opie said, "if they have a solar still."

"But we don't have a 'solar still,' whatever that is," I reminded him.

My confusion must have been written on my face, because he went on to explain that you could build a solar still and exactly what we would need to do so. I was so thirsty I was happy to help; he'd had me at "water."

We searched through our pile of salvaged items for what we needed to construct a still. When we turned around, both Checkers and Moonshine had disappeared. I grabbed one of the galvanized buckets. We loaded up the clear plastic sheet, several pairs of leather work gloves, the small shovel needed to dig the hole for the still, and my plastic pop bottle.

We followed the ditch back the way we had come.

"I bet Checkers and Moonshine went back for more of that buffalo grass," I said.

Opie nodded. But when we reached that spot, the horses were not there. The sun was beating down on us, but I had stopped sweating by this time. A thin crust of grit had formed on my upper lip. I licked it off, surprised at how salty it tasted.

"Phhhht," I whistled for Checkers.

He whinnied back, but he was nowhere in sight. I whistled again, listening closer for the direction of his response. We followed the sound past the clump of junipers, across the expanse of buffalo grass. A long, slow rise led us to a row of rocks and boulders that turned out to be a sort of ledge where the earth had given way into a ravine. As we neared the top, we stumbled upon a cleared area with a mound in the center. The mound was covered in river rocks.

"That looks like a grave," I whispered.

"Why are you whispering?" Opie asked.

I shrugged. "Force of graveyard habit, I guess," I said.

Opie rolled his eyes. "I wonder who's buried there? Don't see any marker, other than that handmade wooden cross."

"It'd be hard to say, out here in No Man's Land," I said.

"Maybe it's the grave of the Man with Two Names," Opie said. He glanced from side to side. "Randall said he still haunts where the town of Mesa used to be."

"You think that's near here?"

"Aren't we near Black Mesa? Isn't it that flat-topped hill in the distance?" Opie pointed west.

"A chill just ran up my spine," I said.

"Me, too," Opie said.

"Look," I said, pointing. "Down there."

Our two horses had grazed their way down a rocky funnel-like depression and now stood in the shade of a large cottonwood tree. Opie and I hiked down the rugged path that wound to the bottom.

"Why do you think they came down here?" I asked.

"Maybe they smelled water," Opie said. "Cottonwoods tend to grow along riverbanks."

"It's too dry and rocky for water. The trees look dead."

"Unless . . ." Opie said, and stopped. "Look at that!"

The closer we had gotten to the bottom, the narrower the trail had become. I now realized Checkers and Moonshine were nowhere near the bottom of the ravine. The nearer we got to them, the more my heart raced. I began to see deeper, past where they had stopped and beyond to a massive rock ledge crawling with vines that almost concealed the opening beneath. "It's a cave!" I hollered.

Opie grinned with pride. *You'd have thought he dug the cave*, I thought. "I bet outlaws used to hang out here," I said.

Opie nodded, and my imagination ran wild. I could see William Coe and his gang camping inside the cave, a man on lookout for the lawmen and vigilantes who chased them. I could picture the outlaw with his rifle at the ready as he peered through the overgrowth hiding the entrance to their lair. Randall had told us all about Coe and his gang on the drive out: how they set up Robbers' Roost near Black Mesa, how they built a stone fortress there to use as their hideout, how eventually they had their own blacksmith shop, gun ports, and a piano, of all things. He had told us other outlaws, like Black Jack Ketchum, also used the hideout.

Opie and I scrambled down the dirt path, passing between some sad looking, half dead trees.

Opie stopped, and pointed at the ground.

"See those wood chips? Beaver." He looked above us at the bare tree limbs and pointed again. "That's where he was gnawing that dead tree."

"Hey, speaking of dead trees, you never said how you lost your leg." The words were no more out of my mouth than my cowboy boots slipped on some loose rocks and I nearly fell. Thoughts of old Bootleg Harlin flashed across my mind. Bootleg Harlin is the namesake of our town, and he got his nickname because he had a wooden leg.

"They don't make prosthetic legs out of dead trees anymore, Dru," Opie said, approaching the opening to the cave.

I set down the bucket. "What you doing?"

"See these long black hairs snagged on this woody vine?"

"Someone else has been here?"

"Yes. Recently, too."

Opie drew aside a tangled curtain of vines. We stuck our heads in and listened. Opie looked at me with raised eyebrows. I gave him a quick nod of approval. With that, we both stepped inside the cool, darkened space. The relief of going from blistering heat and parched ground to the cool, moist air of that cavern was like jumping into Winterhalter Creek after a dusty roundup.

A narrow beam of light pierced the darkness, and I could see that this was no small cave. Opie trained his flashlight beam on the ceiling, which must have been twenty feet above our heads.

"Where'd you get that flashlight," I asked.

"I carry it on the chain with my medical dog tag," Opie said. "Never leave home without it."

"Why am I not surprised?" I said.

Opie panned the interior of the huge cavern with the light beam. He stopped when he got to a ring of singed rocks.

"A fire ring," he said. "A good sign that this cave does not fill up with water."

Opie shone the beam of light against the back of the cave and inched forward. When he moved, I followed. The slick wet bumps in the stone floor caused us to slip and slide and kept us from going very far, very fast for fear of falling.

In the nearly pitch-black space, Opie was barely a shadow in front of me. And then he disappeared.

Chapter 12

Mr. Busy Beaver

"**O**PIE!" I SHOUTED. "Opie?"

"Watch that next step!" He sounded like he was far far away.

"Are you okay?" I hollered.

"Yeah, I'm okay, but there's a drop-off right in front of you. A pretty good one," Opie said.

All I could see was a pinpoint of light from below. "Wait a minute," I said. "I'm going to slip off my belt and maybe you'll be able to reach it."

I knelt, wrapped one end of the belt around my hand, and then dangled the other end over the edge.

"Here you go," I said.

Opie flashed me with the light. I felt him grab the belt buckle. I waited for him to get a solid grip on the thing. He gave it a tug to let me know he was ready, and I leaned back and held it taut as Opie climbed up the side, and out.

"Wow!" I said. "I thought I'd lost you. Is your leg okay?"

"Oh yeah. My new leg is ten times stronger than my old one," Opie said, with a shrug.

"Really?"

"Yeah, I ride horses don't I? Do everything you do don't I?"

"True. True."

"We need more light than this nano beam," Opie said.

"I'm sure we have bigger flashlights in the cattle trailer. We should get back, anyway," I said, feeding my belt back through the loops on my jeans. I was surprised at myself for not being more tempted to explore the cave some more. Guess I'd had enough excitement for one day.

We exited the way we had come until we found ourselves back in the scorching heat of the midday sun. As we retraced our steps, Opie suddenly halted, and I saw him stuff something into the bucket. "We can thank Mr. Busy Beaver for providing these wood chips for kindling," Opie said.

"Oh man, now that's what I'm talking about."

"What?"

"Everything was going along great, and then you have to say something my little brother would say."

"Like what?"

I took the bucket. "That Mr. Busy Beaver baloney."

We scooped up several more handfuls each of the chips and added them into the bucket.

"Didn't mean to offend you."

"There you go, again. Now you sound like my mom!"

I shook my head in exasperation, but as I turned I did see that, lucky for us, Moonshine and Checkers still dozed in the scant shade of the cottonwood tree.

"Never mind. Let's get out of here," I said.

Chapter 13

Desperate Times Call for Desperate Measures

OPIE GRABBED Moonshine's bridle and led him up the winding path. I tugged Checkers into motion, behind them.

"I was thinking," I said, once we reached a level spot, "that going into that cave was like opening the door on an air-conditioned room and, if we could get Randall and Zane down there, it would be more comfortable for them."

"True," Opie said.

We rode our horses back to what had become a make-shift camp while we were gone. On one side, Bo and Cash had strung the tarp from tree branches, draping it over a pair of eight-foot-tall fence panels and anchoring the tail flap with rocks. They had devised a corral for the calves around a scrub oak tree out of more of the portable fence panels. The animals stood like black-and-white dominos in the splotches of shade cast by the branches.

Randall and Zane were leaning up against each other with their backs to the blackjack tree trunk. Both were snoring—Randall loud enough to cut wood. I expected to see Bo and Cash pop out any minute from some hiding spot, but they proved nowhere to be found.

"Wonder where they got to?" I said.

"They'll be back." Opie said as he dismounted and reached for the bucket of odds and ends and wood chips. I handed it over and slid to the ground, as well.

"I'm going to check on Randall and Zane," I said. I jogged over to where the two men were propped against the tree. I touched Zane's boot with mine. He stirred, and his movement woke Randall. "Just checking on you."

"Thanks, Dru," Randall said.

"No problem."

I rejoined Opie and said, "They seem to be okay."

Meanwhile, Opie had taken out a pair of work gloves and the small shovel from the bucket, chosen a spot in direct sunlight, and started digging what looked to be hole.

"Now, the purpose of a solar still," he said as he dug, "is to cause moisture to evaporate, condense water vapor, and then collect the drinkable result."

"In plain English?"

"We're going to pee in this hole. We'll cover it with that clear plastic sheet and use a rock to weight the middle. With the help of the sun, the pee will evaporate and create water vapor. The water vapor will condense on the underside of the plastic.

"If we do this right, the now clean water will run down into that pop bottle. You're going to need to empty the pop out of it, and then cut off the neck to give us a better shot at collecting the drinkable result."

"Pee in what?" Bo asked, as he and Cash came up from behind.

"Where have you guys been?" I asked. "You left Zane and Randall alone! They were asleep when we got back!"

"One of the calves got out," Bo said. "We were only gone a minute."

"Okay, well, sorry," I said. "Didn't mean to bite your head off."

"It's okay," Bo said. "I know we're all a bit on edge. So what are you guys up to?"

I passed out work gloves, while Opie explained the theory behind our project. I took the first turn digging the hole.

"Guess what we found," I said, as I dumped another shovelful of dirt onto the pile. "A cave."

"Where?" Bo asked.

"Actually, Checkers and Moonshine led us to it," Opie said.

"Yeah, they went looking for water, is my guess," I said. "We followed them into a ravine over that way." I pointed in the direction Opie and I had come from. "The cave was at the end hidden by vines. It's huge!"

Our discovery didn't trigger the response I expected. Cash and Bo just stood there.

"I could use some water," Cash said.

"Me, too," Bo said. "I'm parched! Sorry, Dru, all I can think about is how much I want a glass of water right now."

I nodded. That made sense. Dehydration was no laughing matter.

"We all could," I said. "The cave can wait. Let's pee us some drinking water."

With that I handed the shovel to Cash. "Your turn." Bo and Cash looked at me like I was a crazy man. I could tell they weren't too sure about this solar still thing, but, to their credit, they didn't argue. Cash dug the hole down deeper and passed the shovel to Bo. Opie finished it up. The hole ended up about a yard wide and twenty inches deep.

"Okay, guys, time to do our duty," Opie said.

"Oh man, that's gross," Cash said.

"Yeah, it's going to stink," Bo said, making a face.

"Are you sure about this, Opie?" I said.

"Desperate times call for desperate measures. Where else are we going to find water out here in the middle of nowhere?"

With that, Opie unzipped his jeans and peed into the ditch. We all watched dumbstruck. Opie wasn't having it.

"Come on guys. We're wasting valuable time," he said.

Cash, Bo, and I swapped glances.

"You're making this more difficult than it needs to be," Opie said.

"You're right," Bo said. "We need water. This is a way to get water. We're all in this together. Come on Bulldoggers, it's time to man up."

Bo stepped to the ditch, and so did we.

I was surprised to see how fast the dry earth soaked up the pee. I emptied the pop bottle and cut the top off with my pocketknife. I stuck the bottle into the middle of the shallow pond we had made.

Each of us grabbed a corner of the plastic sheet and spread it over the top. We piled stones on the corners. Opie placed an egg-sized rock in the center of the sheet and pushed it down about ten inches into the ditch, enough to create a low point. The center point was directly over the pop bottle. We piled soil, from the hole we had dug, around the edges of the plastic sheet to seal it.

One solar still completed and primed, we stood staring at it as if we might be able to see it produce the first glass of water before our very eyes. Opie quickly nixed that idea.

"This could take a while," Opie said. "In the meantime, let's see what we can find to eat around here."

Chapter 14
Beggars Can't Be Choosers

UNDER THE TREE Randall and Zane stirred and moaned. "Do we have any aspirin?" "Sure thing, Dad," Bo said, "but we don't have any water for you to take it with."

"That's okay. I'll just chew 'em."

"Maybe we should get that ladder and lower it into the ditch. You boys can form a bucket brigade of sorts. Bring all that gear up here. Can't tell when that arroyo will flood again. The storm sending the water could happen up in the mountains, hundreds of miles away," Randall said.

Bo handed Zane two aspirins; he popped them in his mouth and started chewing.

"I don't know how you can do that," Bo said, looking at his father chew. "They taste nasty."

"If your head was throbbing the way mine is, trust me, you would not care how bad they tasted. Not if you knew it would take away some of the pain," Zane said

Randall sat up and put his hand to his forehead. "Whew! I have a doozy of a headache, too, but I think my ankle may hurt more."

"Bo, why don't you go ahead and give a couple of those aspirin to Randall," Zane said. "That is if he doesn't mind having to take them without water."

"I can handle that," Randall said. "Sorry I'm not much help right now."

"Hey neither of us is in very good shape," Zane said. "Luckily we have the boys."

"You need to rest," Randall said, "but it would seem you're improving. You boys go ahead and get that ladder into the ditch and haul that gear up where it will be safe."

"I don't think we need a ladder," Bo said. "I saw some big ole rocks or something sticking out of the bank. We might be able to climb down."

"Let's go look," I said. I followed Bo over to where the road had washed out.

"I didn't notice them until I got down there," Bo said, "but see those big white rocks? They almost look like giant bones."

I leaned over to see what he was talking about. "Wow, I never even noticed that, Bo. I don't think we should walk on them because I think you are right. They do like look like giant bones but not from any animal I've ever seen."

"What are you looking at?" Opie called. He and Cash had moseyed over and now peered into the ditch.

"We think bones," Bo said. "Big old bones. Maybe prehistoric bones."

"You mean like dinosaur bones? I don't know about that," I said. "Probably buffalo or bear."

"I don't know," Bo said. "They're really big. Biggest I've ever seen, except in a museum. But you're probably right, maybe, they're just elk bones. But let's use the ladder anyway, just in case."

Bo went into the trailer and unhooked the ladder from the front. He carried it over to the edge of the ditch. I helped him to lower and lean it against the bank.

He followed me down the ladder back into the ditch, while Cash and Opie stayed at ground level. I passed the items over one by one to Bo, who stood on the ladder and handed them up one by one to the other two.

Cash and Opie took the items and placed them under the tarp, to one side. Sleeping bags, buckets, tools, flashlights and batteries, coolers, water jugs, ropes, extra clothes, and anything else we had salvaged after the truck flipped.

"Most of the food from the cooler is spoiled," Opie said, as he climbed down the ladder into the ditch with me and Bo. "Got too hot . . ."

". . . and covered with ants," I added.

"Hey, they just add a little more protein," Opie said.

"What do? The ants?" Bo said.

"Yeah." Opie leaned over, picked up a piece of bread, and brushed off the dirt. "I know it's not very appetizing, but a little dirt won't hurt us, neither will a few ants." He picked up the plastic bread bag and stuffed the slice of bread back inside. "Give me a hand, will you?"

We collected the scattered slices of bread, brushed them off, and put them in the bag.

"I don't trust the bologna after being in this heat more than an hour, but these pickles should be safe to eat," Opie said.

"Yum. Bread and pickles for dinner," Bo said.

"I can think of worse things," Opie said.

A scene from a *National Geographic* special flashed in my head. People were eating live grubworms. Just the thought made me shudder. "Me, too," I said.

We climbed out of the ditch and carried the bread and pickles over to our new campsite.

"We are going to scout for more food," Opie said.

"That's a good idea," Zane said. "Neither Randall or I are in any condition to be of much help, I'm afraid."

"Dad, you guys just relax," Bo said. "We will take good care of you two. Don't fret none."

"Thank you, son."

"And look what I found," Bo said. "The mystery you were reading on the drive. I found it about twenty feet from the pickup, in the dirt."

Zane took the book, shook the dirt off it, and turned it over in his hands. "Doesn't look any worse for the wear," he said, with a grin. "Great invention, the book."

"That should keep you entertained while we're off scouting for food," Bo said.

"That it will," Zane said. "Thank you, boys."

With that, we each picked up a bucket, and with our gloves shoved into our back pockets, set off in search of anything edible the Oklahoma Panhandle had to offer.

Bo picked up a stick. "This here is my rabbit stick," he said. "In case I run across a jackrabbit."

Bo could hit anything with his catch rope. I had no doubt, if he had a shot at a rabbit, that we would be having *Hasenpfeffer*, otherwise known as rabbit stew, for dinner tonight.

"What do you plan to do with that stick?" Cash said.

"I'm going to throw it," Bo said.

"I haven't seen any critters, but that's probably because

they're smart enough to sleep in the heat of the day," I said.

"There are other things to eat that don't take naps," Opie said.

"Like what?" I asked.

"Things like prickly pear cactus and piñon pine nuts."

"Can't say I have ever eaten those before," Cash said, turning up his nose.

"Beggars can't be choosers," I reminded him.

"I wish I'd thought to bring my atlatl," Opie said.

"What's an *att* . . . an *antl* . . ."

"*Aht-lah-tuhl* is how you say it," Opie repeated, slowly, one syllable at a time. "It's a prehistoric spear-thrower."

"Isn't that used to hunt larger game, like deer?" Bo said.

"Yeah, but it would have been cool just to throw for practice out here."

"I don't know why anyone would ever want to bring an *atla* . . . a primitive weapon to a rodeo in the first place," I said. "And why are we wasting good energy and daylight talking about it when we should be figuring out how we are going to get Randall and Zane to a doctor?"

Opie and Bo exchanged a look.

"We need water and food first," Bo said, "or we will all be needing a doctor. Speaking of which, I have been meaning to say thank you, Opie, for taking care of my dad the way you did back there."

"Aw, it was nothing," Opie said.

"How did you know to do all that stuff?"

This time Opie and I exchanged glances. "I asked him the same thing," I said. "You are not going to believe his answer." I clapped Opie on the back. "Go on, tell him; it's okay. We are all Bulldoggers here."

Opie sighed. "A couple of years back I had a run in with

a lawn mower," he said. "I ended up losing my left leg."

"He has a fake leg!" I said. "He's like the Bionic Man."

"I want to see it," Bo demanded.

Opie made a face and pulled up his pant leg past his boot. "It's made of carbon-fiber."

"Cool, I've seen guys play football wearing those," Bo said.

"I've seen soldiers from the Iraq and Afghanistan wars who lost their legs in explosions wearing them," Cash said.

Opie pulled his pant leg down over his boot. "Now, those prickly pear cactus won't be hard to find. They're everywhere. Lucky for us, the fruit is in season."

"So, it doesn't hurt when you climb on Moonshine, or jump off, or run?" Bo was not ready to let the leg thing go.

"What helps is I still have my own knee. I only lost the lower portion of my leg. The skin can get irritated and it can hurt some. I have ways of fixing those problems when they happen, like this special protective lotion I use."

Opie drew up short. We had come to an area with lots of prickly pear cactuses. Before we could stop him, Cash picked up one of the fruits only to pull back with a shriek. "Ouch!"

"They bite," Opie said. "You need to wear a glove to protect yourself from the prickly part. Hence, the gloves . . ."

He handed one to Cash.

"You could have warned me," Cash whined.

Bo, Opie, and I ignored him. Gloves on, we concentrated on picking the purple fruits and stowing them in the bucket.

"How are we going to eat them?" Cash asked, in between sucking on his sore fingers.

"We can either roll them in sand or gravel to rub off the spines, or we can scorch the spines off in the fire. Then, we split them down the middle and eat them like a grapefruit," Opie said.

"Do they taste like grapefruit?" Bo asked hopefully.

"Nope," Opie said.

"Do they taste like chicken?" I asked, with a big grin.

Opie just shook his head and rolled his eyes.

"I think I'll hold out for something better," Cash said.

With our buckets full of several servings of prickly pear cactuses, Opie led us into a small grove of funny-shaped trees. They reminded me of bonsai trees.

"What's that smell?" I asked, scrunching my nose.

"Piñon pine," Opie said. "We can eat the nuts; they are high in protein and oils. The needles can be made into a tea high in vitamin C."

"I don't like tea," Cash whined.

"Is there anything you do like?" I said, and gave him a warning eye.

"I want a hot dog and a pop," he said.

"That would be nice," Bo said, "but do you see anywhere around here that remotely looks like a Dixie Dog or a Sonic? And, by the way, you do know what the first rule of road tripping is, don't you Cash?"

Cash looked clueless.

"No complaining!" Bo and I said in unison.

Cash just made a face.

While Bo and Cash bickered over the likelihood of finding a drive-in in No Man's Land, I followed Opie's lead. When I found a pine cone, I added it to one of the buckets.

Time passed in almost peaceful quiet when I noticed Cash had wandered a ways from the group. He stood on a humongous boulder. A strong southerly wind threatened to knock him off. He had braced himself with his legs, planting them a shoulder's width apart. He was shielding his eyes from the sun, staring off into the distance.

"Hey guys!" he suddenly shouted. "Water! I've found water!"

Bo, Opie, and I ran to the boulder and scrambled up the side of it. Shielding our own eyes from the sun, we gazed across the vast land spreading before us. Sure enough, there, in the distance, a shallow pond surrounded by lush reeds and cattails sparkled in the sunshine.

My mouth watered at the sight.

"That's an old buffalo wallow," Opie said.

"An old what?" Cash said.

"See how it looks kind of shallow and those plants around it look different from the ones growing in the field or what we see by the pond at home?"

"I guess."

"Well, when the buffalo herds roamed wild, they would wallow in the dust to give themselves a coat of dirt to protect themselves from fleas and ticks. Then in the spring they wallowed to shed their winter coats."

We climbed down and crossed the field of buffalo grass.

"The oil and fur from their coats mingled with the dust and, as you know, buffalo weigh as much as a compact car. With that much body weight, they hard-packed that dirt and created big depressions in the prairie where water could collect, as we have here."

Opie knelt and pulled out some cattails by the roots.

"We can use everything on these from the roots to the pollen heads. The roots can be eaten raw or steamed. We can use the pollen to thicken stew if Bo is lucky enough to get us that jackrabbit," Opie said.

"How long do you think we're going to be stuck out here?" I asked. "I don't know about you, but I'm not interested in playing survival campout."

"Like it or not, Dru," Bo said, "we are out here with no way to get hold of help for now. The way I figure it, though, Scotty and his mom are expecting us home. When we don't show up, they will send out a search party."

"Yeah, but they aren't expecting us home till late, Sunday," I said. "And Randall said he didn't take the usual route because of the weather forecast. He was trying to make better time."

"No irony there," Bo said.

"My point is we are looking at the chance of ugly storms coming this way, and there is no telling how long it will take for someone to find us," I said.

"Stop!" Opie yelled.

I thought he was mad at me for going on and on about our predicament, and it shocked me. I'd never heard Opie raise his voice before. But then I saw he was running after Cash. Cash, who was now lying on his stomach by the buffalo wallow.

"Stop!" Opie hollered again.

But he was too late. Cash was face down in the water, drinking it by the handful.

We followed Opie, yelling as we ran. Cash finally stood up. Water dripped from his chin. His clothes were soaked.

"That water isn't safe to drink," Opie said, between trying to catch his breath.

"Couldn't help myself," Cash said. "I was dying of thirst."

Chapter 15
Team Work

BEFORE WE GOT back to camp with buckets full of water from the buffalo wallow for the livestock, Cash's belly was already cramping. I have to say he was a trooper—he even helped to water the calves. Then the vomiting began.

Every time he heaved, I wanted to toss my cookies, too. Something about the sound of throwing up brings on the same urge in me. Call it sympathy retching, I guess. After a while, Cash curled up in a ball on one of the horse blankets.

As bad as I felt for Cash, with a water source handy, my mood had vastly improved. I did not even mind when Opie asked me and Bo to gather tinder.

"We have cattail down," he said, "and dead agave stalks make great coal carriers—the inner wood is incredibly soft and can be lit with just flint and steel. Maybe get some dry pine needles, too, and dried flood debris from along the ditch."

"Don't forget those wood chips we found, compliments of Mr. Beaver," I said.

Opie smiled. I could tell he knew I was trying.

"The wood chips will be good for kindling," Opie said. "Look for thin dry branches and plant stalks up to a pencil-round in thickness. And dry wood. Dead tree branches, not on the ground. Get it from standing trees, alive or dead."

"I saw a bunch of dead trees and branches down by the cave," I told Bo.

"Cool, I was wanting to see that cave, anyway," Bo said.

"This is no time to go exploring," Opie said, putting his hands on his hips.

I rolled my eyes.

"Don't roll your eyes at me."

"I'll roll my eyes if I feel like it," I said. *How quickly I back-slide*, I thought. I stepped closer to Opie and put my hands on my hips.

"Hold on, guys," Bo said, stepping between us. "That's dehydration talking. Let's just go, Dru."

He pulled me away by the arm.

"We'll be back as fast as we can, Opie," he said.

* * * * * *

By the time Bo and I returned to camp, Opie had already spread the pine cones out in the sun to dry. He had cleared a flat area and built a fire ring out of rocks. Inside the fire ring, he had started to dig a hole. He was working on that when Randall called us all over.

Bo and I dropped what we had in our arms on the ground. Opie followed.

"Listen, guys," Randall said. "You're doing a great job of taking charge and getting things done. Opie, I know you are one skilled camper. However, our first priority must be clean water for us to drink."

Opie explained the wallow of water Cash had found and sampled.

"Well that's fine for the stock," Randall said, "but it won't do the horses or us any good unless we boil it."

"We still have the solar still," I said.

Randall looked confused.

"While you and Zane were resting, we built a solar still to get potable drinking water," Opie explained. "But that will take some time. Meanwhile, I thought I might as well dig a keyhole fire pit so we can cook that jackrabbit when Bo catches it."

"I'm sure I can scare one up, given half a chance," Bo said.

"No doubt, you would catch it, too," Randall said. "But I don't know if that will be necessary. I expect they're going to be sending out a search party for us as soon as either the rodeo folks or Arlene figure out we're missing."

"How long do you think that'll take?" Bo asked.

"Hard to say," Randall said. He ran a hand through his hair. "To be honest, maybe, we do need to be prepared to spend a few nights out here. If so, we definitely need a good fire going."

"I was afraid you were going to say that," Bo said.

"We're going to be here a few nights?" I said.

"That's not to say we will be," Randall said, "but we need to be prepared to be, just in case. You'll be surprised, when that sun sets, how fast it'll cool down, so we need to have bedrolls made before it gets too dark. As hot and sweaty as we are right now, you'll be glad to have something to cover up with, later. The fire is our first priority, though. We will need rocks for boiling the water, too, now that you boys found a water source."

Cash moaned and crawled off behind the tree. Bo and I looked dubiously at Randall, but Opie seemed to take what he had to say in stride.

"Once we build the fire, we can look for rocks," Opie said.

The three remaining vertical Bulldoggers began constructing a fire. We opted for one in the distinctive cone shape of a tipi because we have been building tipi camp fires from the time we were old enough to help gather wood. Granted, under normal circumstances, we would have had everything needed at hand to do so. This time, we'd have to improvise.

A tipi fire is the best design for a fire because it can burn all by itself without anyone having to stoke it. That's because as it burns, it falls inward and feeds itself.

We piled a good amount of dried grass in the center of the fire ring. Next, from the tinder and kindling Bo and I had collected earlier, we selected a handful of foot-long pieces. Bo took them in both hands and, with thumbs down, broke them in the middle. He stood them up on end like tipi poles, using his thumbs to create a doorway. He faced the opening to the wind in order to help spread the fire into the tipi, once it was lit.

I layered on more kindling and smaller pieces of wood. Together we kept adding more and more wood of larger sizes. We held off on the fattest logs until we could get some good coals going. Add big logs too early and we risked snuffing out the fire before it had a chance to get going.

Opie pulled out his neck chain again. This time, he removed his flint and steel from it.

Boy that kids comes prepared, I couldn't help thinking.

Opie knelt plucked some tufts of down from the head of one of the cattails and tucked it inside the dried buffalo and blue grama grasses we had used as our first layer of tinder. He struck the steel on the flint over and over trying to get a spark to ignite the cattail down, with no luck.

"I don't know why it won't light," he said.

I could tell he was frustrated and thirsty, as we all were.

Zane carefully reached in his back pocket and pulled out a butane lighter.

"Haven't smoked in years," he said, "but I feel naked without this dang thing."

He handed it to Opie.

Opie smiled. It was the first smile any of us had seen in a while.

Chapter 16
A Watched Pot Never Boils

OPIE LIT THE cattail down. The flame ignited the pile of dried grass. Before long, the pencil-thick sticks caught fire. We all smiled then. With the fire lit and burning well, Bo, Opie, and I set out to find rocks before it got dark. We split up, each going our own way. We came back with our pockets bulging and our arms full, and set our rocks down in the fire.

"It will take about forty-five minutes for those rocks to be glowing hot," Randall said. "In the meantime, we can strain the grit out of the water. It's best to do it at least twice. We need to find a clean pair of blue jeans and a T-shirt to use as a sieve. We also need tongs or a ladle or something to scoop the rocks out of the fire."

Bo and I dug around in our bags until we found the required jeans and the T-shirt. Bo fit the jeans over one bucket, while I stretched the T-shirt over another. Opie found a soup ladle. I poured water from one bucket through the jeans, into a bucket underneath. I was surprised to see so much silt collect on top. We then poured the strained water into the bucket with the T-shirt stretched over it.

We were repeating the process with the second bucket of water when suddenly we were under attack.

Bang! Bang! Bang!

We dove to the ground and covered our heads until the shooting stopped.

"Okay, who got the wet rocks?" Zane hollered.

I raised my head and saw Zane standing by the fire. No gunmen in sight. Nonetheless, I thought his a particularly silly question to ask with shots being fired.

"I said, who got the wet rocks?" Zane said. "And for goodness sakes get up, it's plenty safe—that wasn't gunfire."

We all got to our feet. The other Bulldoggers looked at me. No one had yet answered his question.

"It was me, sir," I said stepping forward. "I found them in the buffalo wallow."

Zane nodded. "Wet rocks explode when heated as the moisture turns to steam. If there's enough room for pressure to build, it blows up. Sorry I did not think to mention it sooner." He rubbed his forehead with the palm of his hand. "Just darn lucky no one got hurt from it. They might not be bullets, but I can attest they hurt if they hit you."

The guys and I swapped glances and went back to work. I picked up the second bucket and continued pouring the water through the jeans. Bo poured the strained water into the next bucket, through the T-shirt, and so forth.

"Would you bring that ladle over here, Opie. The rest of those rocks are glowing red now," Zane said.

Opie scooped an egg-sized rock from the coals and blew

off as much of the ash as he could. He placed the hot rock in the first bucket of strained water. He continued moving rocks until he had about eight hot rocks in each bucket full of water. The three of us watched intently, waiting for something to happen.

"Don't you boys know that a watched pot never boils?" Zane said, with a chuckle.

"Whoever said that never used hot rocks," Bo said. "That pot's boiling already."

Chapter 17
What Do You Mean by Tainted?

ONCE THE WATER had boiled for a while, we poured it into one of our containers to cool. Bo and I returned to the buffalo wallow and refilled four buckets with water so we could do it all over again. We carried the heavy water buckets back to camp.

While we waited for the hot water to cool, Opie showed us how to pop piñon nuts from the dried pine cones. We had decided to save them for a snack, later. Bo collected them in his bandanna.

"I wonder how the solar still is doing," I said.

"Oh yeah," Opie said. "Let's go check it out."

Bo and Cash followed us to the still. Opie squatted to get a closer look at the pop bottle. He made a face, then stood and held up the pop bottle so we could see inside. Water barely covered the bottom.

"Well, I guess, I learned a lesson from this," Opie said.

"What's that?" Cash said.

"If you need water, don't build a solar still unless you have a lot of time to wait for it to work."

"I have to admit," I said, "it does make me appreciate indoor plumbing more."

We wandered back to the campfire ready for our snack. We each sharpened a stick with our pocket knives and then poked it through several of the prickly pear fruits. We roasted them over the fire like marshmallows but only long enough to burn off the spines.

Next Zane showed us how to use our knives to split them open on a flat rock and peel out the meat. It tasted juicy, sweet, and delicious—like eating pears, watermelon, beets, and berries all at the same time.

Now it was time for some water. Finally. We added apple flavoring to one of the water jugs and gave it to the horses. Then, we took turns filling the ladle and drinking. The water was warm and tasted muddy, but no one seemed to care. If it could have, my tongue would have done a backflip when the wetness hit it, it was so happy.

"Dad," Bo said, "how come Cash got sick from that water? I mean, I know it has dirt in it, but we all ate dirt when we were little. And how come the livestock can drink it without it making them sick?"

Zane passed a ladle of water to Cash, who had gathered strength enough to join our circle. Zane ruffled Cash's hair.

"Yeah," Cash said. "I figured since it was rain water, it would be okay."

"Where exactly did you get the water?" Zane asked.

"From an old buffalo wallow," Cash said.

"In that case," Zane said, "you definitely had no business drinking that water—it's tainted."

"What do you mean 'tainted'?" Cash said.

"It means it's dirty. That's typical of stagnant water that doesn't flow. No stream or creek feeds fresh water into it, so it is easy for it to go bad, but even in a free-flowing stream the water can be tainted with bacteria from animal feces, or poop, that our guts just can't handle—E. coli and hepatitis, parasites and flatworms.

"Horses have a more sensitive palate than cattle. That's why we started adding apple flavoring to their water a week before this trip. Otherwise, they would not drink strange water. Their sense of smell protects them. Cattle, on the other hand, drink stagnant water from the time they are born, and so they have the tough digestive tract to handle it."

Zane poked the fire with his stick and grimaced.

"What now?" Bo asked.

"Well, nowadays, we also have to worry about chemicals and toxins—PCBs, heavy metals, growth hormones, runoff from poultry farms, even chemicals from soap. They can all get in the water and pollute it. Then there is the occasional algae bloom that can carry the bacteria that causes cholera."

"You're making my stomach hurt again," Cash said, rubbing his tummy.

"You were very lucky, Cash," Zane said. "As bad as that water made you feel, it could have been a lot worse. It could have killed you."

The look on Cash's face said he heard Zane loud and clear.

"But it didn't," Zane said, smiling. "I think you're just worn out from being sick, hungry, and dehydrated. And we can fix at least two of those things right now. The pickles will restore our electrolytes and the bread will make us feel full."

"Let's eat!" We said in unison, well, all of us save for Cash. At the mention of food, his face had turned pickle green.

Chapter 18
Lucky Us

WE ALL FELT BAD for Cash and his upset stomach, really we did. But it was Opie who came to the rescue again with a simple remedy he remembered from another camping trip. Who would guess that charcoal could be such a lifesaver?

Cash had a few licks of a charred stick from the fire, and his stomach settled down enough for him to realize just how homesick he was.

Poor kid cried himself to sleep.

I think we were all struggling with homesickness on some level or other. I could only imagine how badly Randall wanted out of No Man's Land, what with his ankle hurt and his shoulder messed up. Not to mention his brand new pickup, being totaled.

As the rest of us sat around the campfire, our bellies somewhat satisfied, lost in our own thoughts, Randall cleared his throat. We all turned to look at him.

"We've been mighty lucky today," he said.

I raised my eyebrows. "Lucky?"

"Yes."

"How could wrecking the truck be lucky?" Bo asked.

"We've had some discomfort and misfortune, I'll grant you," Randall said, "but we're all still alive. Cash could have been much worse. Zane and I could have been much worse. And you other boys could have been injured in the crash."

"The truck couldn't be much worse," I said.

Everyone chuckled at that.

"None of the animals were injured, either," Opie said.

"And we didn't get that bad weather Zane was worried about," I said.

"Well, the verdict is still out on that one," Randall said. "I keep telling you, the weather out here can change in an instant. It's left cowboys more seasoned than us scrambling for their lives."

The fire crackled and popped. The sun crept closer to the horizon, setting the sky aglow with pinks and reds and blues and purples. A coyote howled in the distance. As the sun slipped away, a calm settled over us.

"Of course, that's true anywhere in Oklahoma," Zane said. "Think about those folks around Moore last May."

"Those storms popped up out of nowhere," I said.

"People hardly had time to take cover!" Opie said.

"Did you realize," Randall said, "it wasn't until 1948 that two men working at Oklahoma's Tinker Air Force Base in Midwest City issued the first tornado warning. Those men saved who knows how many lives. Before that, people thought tornadoes defied prediction."

"What does that mean?" Cash asked, sitting up.

86

"Well, sleepyhead," Randall said, "it means no one had paid close enough attention to the right things. For as long as anyone could remember, there had been no scientific agreement as to how to tell where or when a tornado would drop out of the sky.

"Today it's its own science. We have storm chasers driving Doppler on Wheels, or DOWs; they carry Doppler radar equipment, which can detect when conditions exist for a tornado to form. Thousands of lives have been saved by their early warnings."

Randall paused. "What happened in Moore and Carney and Shawnee in May was tragic and heartbreaking. People died, and many others lost their homes and everything they owned. Many folks, however, were able to take shelter, thanks to the warnings of Oklahoma weathermen."

"I heard there were people whose skin was taken off from debris hitting them," Cash said.

"I heard there was a school teacher who saved the lives of her students by covering them with her body when the tornado hit," Opie said.

We all got quiet at that. Randall nodded in affirmation. "For all the devastation a tornado can wreak, equally amazing are the ways people come together to help each other through such tragedies."

"This might be a good time to ask if you know what to do if you get caught in such a situation," Zane said.

"We have a fraidy hole behind our house," Cash said.

"We have one at school," Opie said, "I checked on my first day in class."

"That's all well and good," I said, "but what do we do out here? This place is as flat as a piece of paper. There's nowhere to hide."

"That's true," Randall said. "The best thing to do out here is to find the lowest spot—a ditch or Cash's buffalo wallow—lie down flat, cover your head, and hope for the best. Don't stand under a tree. A tree is more likely to get struck by lightning. Always be aware of your surroundings and keep an eye on the sky.

"Even though meteorologists—the people who study the weather—can predict the possibility of severe weather, tornadoes remain unpredictable, especially when it comes to where they will touch down, how strong or wide they will be, or how long they will stay on the ground."

"Yeah," Opie said, "I've heard tell of how after a tornado hits, the walls and the roof of a house will be gone, but the kitchen table will be left right where it was, with dinner dishes still on it. But I have also heard of entire neighborhoods being laid flat like in Moore."

"That's why," said Randall, "my advice is that if you find yourself facing off with a tornado, the best defense is to go underground."

"Like that cave we found," I said.

"Yes," Randall said, "but if you can't get underground, find the lowest possible spot, lie down, and cover your head—just be careful not to lie in a watercourse, like that arroyo, because flash flooding often accompanies such storms. I know that's probably clear as mud, but it's the best advice I have on the subject."

"I wish there were storm shelters out here," Cash said, looking at the sky.

For the first time on the trip, Cash and I were in complete agreement. I thought about the tornadoes that had steamrolled central Oklahoma last May and I shivered.

Opie must have sensed we were all feeling a little scared

and blue, for he pulled his harmonica from his shirt pocket and set to playing, "This Land Is Your Land." Bo started singing along and pretty soon we all joined in. For a while, I forgot about being sad and scared.

"Does anyone know who wrote that song?" Zane asked, winking at Opie. "Other than Opie, that is."

"John Denver?" Bo said.

"Garth Brooks?" Cash said.

"Nope, it was Woody Guthrie," Zane said. "He was from Oklahoma and lived later in the Texas panhandle during the Dust Bowl. He turned that experience into an album called *Dust Bowl Ballads*."

"Here's one." Opie played another tune. "Recognize it?"

"'So Long, It's Been Good to Know You,'" Bo sang.

"That's right!"

"What's the Dust Bowl?" Cash asked. "It sounds a lot like a college bowl game."

Opie and Zane groaned. Randall shook his head in wonder. I bit back a smart comment. It fell to Zane to set him straight.

"Well, Cash," Zane said, "the Dust Bowl had nothing to do with college football and everything to do with a terrible drought that hit part of the United States in the 1930s. They also called it the Great Plow-up. Farmers had plowed all the grasslands in order to plant wheat, and the lack of rain combined with all that soil exposed to the wind created dust storms the likes of which had never been seen before. It lasted ten years! That's almost your whole lifetime! People lost everything. The farmers couldn't grow any crops. The farmers' wives couldn't grow their vegetable gardens. And the livestock had nothing to eat, either ... the grass turned to dirt."

"Where did it happen?" Cash asked.

"Right here in Oklahoma. The Oklahoma Panhandle was among the worst area hit of all the surrounding states. But Kansas suffered a lot, too. As did Texas," Zane said.

Opie picked that moment to play "Home on the Range," and soon all the Bulldoggers were singing. When he moved on to the theme song of the old television western *Rawhide*, Randall and Zane smiled and joined in. I'd forgotten how catchy the song was as we sang "rolling, rolling, rolling" clear through to the end.

As the last note faded away in the night, Randall said, "I bet you boys don't know where Zane's name comes from."

"I figured it had something to do with Zane Grey, the western novel writer," Opie said.

"Well, yes, that's part of it," Zane said. "May I?"

"Of course," Randall said.

"It is kind of a funny story," Zane said. "I don't know if you boys realize that Randall and I have been friends forever, sort of the way you two," he pointed at Bo and me, "have been friends since birth.

"Randall's parents and my parents were best friends, too. They got together every week to watch reruns of *Zane Grey Western Theatre*, and it just so happened that one of the spin-off shows from that television series called *Wanted: Dead or Alive* starred Steve McQueen as U.S. Marshall Josh Randall. So, when we were born, we didn't stand a chance."

"I had forgotten that, Dad," Bo said.

"Yeah, our names were inspired by TV," said Zane.

He and Randall got a good laugh out of that.

"I think that's the first time I've heard either of you really laugh since the wreck," I said.

"On that note, you boys should hit the hay," Randall said.

"Mr. Fender, do you mind if I see us out with 'Taps'?"

"What would a campfire be without it," Randall said.

Opie's haunting rendition of "Taps" stayed with me as we contained the fire and found our spots for the night. I could see now how playing the tin sandwich for a restless herd on a long cattle drive through wild, open prairie might be calming, because before long we were all curled up in our sleeping bags dozing off, one by one, to Opie's mournful blues.

Chapter 19
Jackalopes!

I WOKE BEFORE THE sun came up, cold. I tried burrowing deeper into my sleeping bag so my head was covered but then the bag got too hot and steamy inside—*who knew I produced so much hot air*—and I had to uncover. I finally got tired of fooling with it and just climbed out altogether, shoved my feet into my boots, and clamped on my hat. That way, at least, both my feet and my head were warm at the same time.

The fire had nearly died out. I stirred the embers to see if any sparks remained. Bo clambered out of his sleeping bag about this time, and found his boots and hat.

He whispered, "You need some help?"

"Sure."

We set about building a new tipi with the kindling and logs we had left.

Zane got up while we were stacking the fire. "You boys

are up early," he said. "The last time I added wood to the fire was around three o'clock, I think."

"There were some hot embers still left when I woke up just now, but not much heat," I said.

A moan and murmur came from deep within Cash's sleeping bag: "I'm cold . . . and I'm hungry."

Zane and I ignored him. Bo, however, couldn't let it pass.

"Of course, you are," Bo said. "And you just set a record for fastest whine of the day. Congratulations, Cash!"

The sleeping bag went silent.

"What do we have for breakfast?" I asked.

Zane scratched his head. "Pickles, I guess."

Cash's sleeping bag groaned and said: "Piiii-ckkkkk-lessss . . ."—followed by a massive sigh both pathetic and loud enough for us all to hear.

Again, Zane and I ignored it.

Bo mumbled under his breath: "He may not be good at a lot of things, but he is certainly a champion whiner."

"Okay Bo, that's enough," Zane said.

Randall stirred in his sleeping bag. I heard him breathing slow and deep as he first uncovered himself and then sat up. He had to be hurting, no doubt, after a night sleeping on the rock-hard ground.

Opie was the last to rise, but once his eyes opened, his feet were in his boots and he was ready to go. Where he was going, nobody knew. He paced around the campsite in an ever larger circle until it sunk in that there was nowhere else to go. He plopped next to me and started picking at his thumbnail.

Morning light inched up over the horizon, casting a yellow hue across the land.

I heard it before I could see it—movement. The sound

swelled as the sun rose. I held my breath. It was as if we were all paralyzed; our eyes scanned the horizon. A long-eared animal came into focus. He zigzagged across the field and then hopped out of sight. Opie took off after him. He zigged and he zagged, imitating the animal's path.

"Jackalope!" Cash hollered from the warm confines of his sleeping bag. Only his head protruded from the bag—he seemed to have forgotten his hunger for the moment.

"No such thing," Zane said. "There are such animals as antelope jackrabbits. That, however, was a black-tailed jack-rabbit."

Bo stood rooted to the ground, holding his throwing stick. "I managed to grab my stick, but I didn't know where to aim! It happened so fast!"

"Dang, I can almost taste that rabbit stew," Cash said.

"Don't get your taste buds or your stomach in an up-roar," Randall said. "Jackrabbits can go fifty miles per hour when being chased. The chance of Bo catching one was always slim."

"Jackrabbits became so numerous here during the Dust Bowl, folks would organize jackrabbit drives, or hunts," Zane said. "They'd post flyers saying whose farm to meet at and when. And fifty families might show up. My father talked about attending one as a boy. He said it was chaos with people yelling, jackrabbits hopping, and kids screaming. Not your ideal hunting party."

"Sort of reminds me of Saturday mornings when all my sons lived at home," Randall said.

Zane chuckled. "Chaos describes it doggone perfectly."

Bo said, "I'm pretty good with this throwing stick, but I don't see me hitting a tiny target like that going fifty miles an hour in a million directions at once."

Opie returned to camp about then, out of breath but just in time to hear Bo. "Maybe there's another way," he said. "I know how to set up a rabbit snare. I bet between our two methods, one or the other will work."

"Hold on, there," Zane said. "We need to discuss something important before we go doing any hunting. You do know the state wildlife department has laws about when you can hunt various animals, right? I know for a fact this is not rabbit season."

"Awwww," we moaned in unison.

"Now wait a minute," Zane said. "Let me finish. I also know, on good authority, that there isn't a game warden in the great state of Oklahoma who would arrest, or even fine, us for hunting a rabbit under these circumstances."

"So," I said, "what you're saying is that since we are stranded out here in No Man's Land, with very little food, if we were to be lucky enough to snare us a jackrabbit or two, nobody would blame us for cooking them for dinner."

"Exactly," Zane said. "Many states, for example Alaska, have what they call subsistence provisions, which is legal talk for saying what Dru just said. Now, I suggest Cash and Bo round up more prickly pears and piñon nuts. Not only will it stave off hunger pangs, but it will give you two something constructive to do."

Cash and Bo each located a pair of gloves and a bucket. Their bickering already forgotten, the two Bulldoggers walked away already hatching a new plan to catch jackrabbits.

I joined Opie at our salvage pile and watched as he picked up a multipurpose tool, then put it back down, picked up a cattle prod—turning it over and over in his hands—before putting it back down, too.

My curiosity got the best of me. "What are you looking for Opie," I asked.

"I need a cord like you would find on a lamp," he said.

"So why do you keep picking up things then putting them right back down again?"

"It helps me to think creatively."

Intrigued, I gave it a try. I picked up a roll of black electrical tape. I turned it over in my hands. I put it down.

"Hey," I said. "Have you seen that light with the hook, the one we use when we're fiddling with the tractor engine?"

"You mean the shop light?" Opie said. "The one with the twenty-five-foot orange cord? That would work. How did you think of that? And, no, I haven't seen it since the wreck."

"I remembered we had to repair a split in it with this electrical tape, last week."

I had to admit Opie's method of puzzling through a problem worked well if my first try was any indication.

"I think we should ask Randall if it's okay to use that cord," Opie said. "If we can find it."

"Good idea, maybe, Randall will know where he last saw it before the crash," I said.

Back at camp, we found Zane and Randall whittling away on what had not too long ago been tree branches.

"What are you guys making?" I asked.

"What does it look like?" Randall said, and held his stick up. It had a point on one end.

"It looks like a tent stake to me," I said.

"Are those for the snare?" Opie said.

Randall looked at Opie. "They certainly are, young man. We'll have a few more ready soon."

Zane looked at Randall. "He guessed that right off, just as you said he would."

Opie beamed. "Thank you, sirs. How did you know what type of snare it would be?"

"Process of elimination," Zane said. "We knew you would need to use a snare that did not require bait."

"And," Randall added, "one that did not require a lot of knowledge of the rabbit's habits. Meaning, where it sleeps, eats, and roams."

"I don't know what to say," Opie said.

"It's the least we could do for the fellow who put my shoulder back in place. I still can't believe you never even hesitated."

"It had to be done quick, or else it might not have gone back together," Opie said, matter-of-factly.

"My point exactly," Randall said.

"I'm afraid I haven't been much help on this trip," Zane said. "Thank goodness some of you have been. Thank you, Opie."

Opie fiddled with the dog tag on his medical chain, eyes on the ground, a little self-conscious.

"We wanted to ask," I said, hopeful I could knock some of the awkwardness out of the moment, "if you know where the shop light is, and if we could we use the cord from it."

"Let me think," Randall said.

He took off his cowboy hat and ran his hand over his short-cropped hair, and then replaced his hat and tapped it down firmly with one fluid movement, as if he had done it a thousand times before—which he had. "I always keep that shop light in the toolbox in the back of the truck."

"Dru thought of using the shop light," Opie said.

"But I would not have thought of it if you hadn't showed me your trick for solving problems," I said.

"What trick?" Randall wanted to know.

97

Opie shoved his hands in his pockets.

"Don't be shy," I said.

"Well, when I don't have exactly what I need to do something, I'll start picking up objects and turning them over . . . and then I kind of let my brain float around the idea of what I might be able to use instead."

"That's very clever and resourceful," Randall said. "Finding ways to use what you have on hand for something other than its original purpose."

"I've never really thought about it before, but my dad does that all the time when he's fixing the tractor," I said.

"That's right. He doesn't always have time to run to town to buy the exact part he needs. Or, if I know your dad as well as I think I do, he doesn't want to spend the money." Randall chuckled.

"So true," I said, and smiled.

I didn't mind the teasing. Randall had known my father for years and I knew he respected him, only trouble was, inside, I was starting to miss my dad. He might run short on cash sometimes, but he has never run short of time for me.

Opie and I took off for the truck. We made a sweep of the area. Like rescue teams searching for a missing person, we started close to the crash site and worked our way out from there, circling the vehicle in an ever widening path.

Opie spotted the cord before I did. He raised it above his head like a trophy he had won, wearing a broad grin on his face. A second later, he was all business again. He pulled the multipurpose tool from his back pocket.

"We better get started."

Chapter 20
Dark Clouds

OPIE AND I set to work stripping the insulation from the cord. Once we had the copper strands exposed, Opie cut them into two-foot-long sections.

"We have enough copper wire here to make plenty of snares," he said.

By that time, Bo and Cash were back in camp with their buckets full of nuts and prickly pears.

"Breakfast!" Cash hollered.

We all gathered round and took a helping of each, carefully, since our fingers were no match for the sharp spines of the prickly pear. Opie spread rags on the ground so he could lay out the piñon nuts from the pine cones to dry.

Zane helped us scorch off the spines from the prickly pears over the fire. No one complained about the meal, not even Cash.

"Full bellies make for much happier campers," Randall

said, after we finished eating. "Now, who wants Zane and me to teach them how to build a snare?"

Five hands went up—Bo was so excited he raised both of his.

"Opie, would you please demonstrate, and then we'll help you each figure out a good spot to place your snare. Placement of the snare is key."

"This morning I was able to watch a momma jackrabbit with her babies," Opie said. "I watched which way she went, so I think I know their territory, sort of. I was kinda surprised at how she just left the babies to fend for themselves though."

"Actually," Randall said, "that has something to do with jackrabbits actually being hares not rabbits. Baby rabbits, or kittens as they are called, are born in nests helpless, naked, and blind, but baby hares, or leverets, are born with a full fur coat, able to see, and capable of living on their own an hour after their birth. That's why your momma jackrabbit wasn't worried about leaving her babies alone in their form."

"Their form?" Cash asked.

"That's what you call a hare's home," Randall said, "but let's get back to the task at hand. Opie, you're up!"

"Yes, sir! Okay Bulldoggers, here are two sections of wire for each of you. Each section has about twenty strands of copper. Twist the strands together on each section, making sure the ends won't come unraveled."

Bo, Cash, and I did as he said, and held up the results.

"Well done," Opie said. "Okay, now make a loop on one end, and crimp it. Slide the other end through the loop."

Opie demonstrated what he meant. Once we had our loops made, he continued.

"I have smaller pieces of wire here to wrap around the wire on the outside of the lasso to keep it from opening up too wide. We need a four-finger-wide loop, four fingers from the ground." He showed us how to measure it with his hand. "Now, we need to attach the snare to one of these stakes Zane and Randall whittled."

Again, Opie demonstrated. We watched carefully as he wrapped the end of the wire around the stake, and then followed suit with our own wire and stakes.

"We'll wait to make the final crimp until we find where we are going to set it, because we'll have to adjust it to suit the location," Opie explained. "I think we're ready to head out."

We followed Zane into the thicket where we had seen the jackrabbit go. Zane showed us how to clutter up the trail alongside our snares with small branches and debris because, as he said, "Animals, like people, are basically lazy, and will take the easiest path."

Zane added, "To detour deer around your trap, you'll need to put a good-sized branch over the top of your snare—deer won't want to step over the branch. They'll go another way."

Each of us set a couple of snares in our own carefully chosen locations. Once the last stake had been angled and stuck in the ground, Zane went back to camp to sit with Randall.

We, on the other hand, did not want to miss any of the action, so we took cover near our snares and waited. And waited. And waited.

The ground underneath me grew harder and harder by the minute. Sweat rolled down my back and my forehead and into my eyes. Flies buzzed my ears and mouth, but still I sat motionless as a statue. Not even a breeze. The air felt heavy and thick in my nose.

My stomach rumbled with hunger so loudly I knew it had to have scared off most of the small game in the area. My mind wandered. I started making bets with myself on who would be the first Bulldogger to give up the watch. I fantasized about how big the jackrabbit would be that got caught in my snare. I thought about how good rabbit would smell cooking on a spit over our campfire. I also dozed off a couple of times, but I did not move. Heck, I barely breathed.

I had my ears tuned for any sound—a rustle of leaves, a twig snapping underfoot.

Then it dawned on me—we weren't going to catch a juicy jackrabbit right now because the whole of the animal kingdom naps during the heat of the day—unlike us, at the top of the food chain with our big brains that cause us to think too much. I nearly laughed out loud at myself and our ignorance.

Before I could call my fellow Bulldoggers off the hunt, I saw something move out of the corner of my eye. A mouse? A snake? I turned to look.

A pronghorn deer stood not far from me, its nose in the wind. I caught the flick of a tail as a round-tailed horned lizard slipped under a rock. Then, a squirrel chattered and a flock of starlings took flight. I looked up and saw storm clouds off in the distance.

I let loose with our secret Bulldogger call: *Bob-white. Bob-white*, I whistled. Today is was supposed to be our signal for if we snagged us a jackrabbit. The other three Bulldoggers hurried over on stiff legs to where I now stood.

"Well, where is it?" Bo asked.

"Did it get away?" Opie said.

"What happened?" Cash said.

"No, no. It's a storm. We have to go. Now!"

With that, I started running for camp. The others fell in right behind me. We were all huffing and puffing by the time we finally made it back to camp. Randall and Zane were dozing, propped against the tree, in the shade of the tarp. The leaves on the treetops fluttered. The tarp rippled and bucked.

"Randall, Zane—storm!" I barely got the words out I was breathing so hard.

Randall and Zane sat up, immediately awake. Already, the wind had picked up. A gust hit the back of my head with the wallop of a massive shop fan turned on high speed. I turned to see Bo's eyes bulging in his head.

"Cloud to ground lightning." He pointed. "Over there."

Zane turned and frowned. "I'm seeing electric lines popping with sparks off in the distance. It seems to be moving this way."

"What is?" Randall said from under the tree.

"Twister."

Chapter 21
Twister!

THE OKLAHOMA PANHANDLE is high by elevation but flat as a dining room table to the eye—you can see anything coming miles and miles away. What we saw wasn't close but it made my stomach drop. And I thought I heard someone whimper in fear.

A massive gray wall cloud moved across the sky, a funnel cloud dangling from it. There was no debris cloud, so it hadn't touched ground, yet, but Zane was right—it was headed straight for us.

Wind whistled across the Great Plains. The sky turned a wicked shade of green, so scary it raised the hairs on the back of my neck.

We starred at the storm as if in a trance. I knew what everyone was thinking, even Randall and Zane: *How could this be happening to us now, after all we had been through? The wreck. Randall's dislocated shoulder. Cash's poisoned stomach. The failure to snag a hare or anything else to eat.* Zane was the first to move.

"Boys, give me a hand," he said.

I marveled at how calm he kept his request. We followed him to the corral. He opened the fence panel.

"Shoo those calves out of there," he said. "Leave the horses."

Bo, Cash, Opie, and I ran around behind the herd of calves. It didn't even take a touch. We just raised our arms and clicked our tongues; the calves were so used to our way of moving them around, they got the picture. When the last calf had left the pen, Zane said, "Be assured, they will find a safe place. It's built into their DNA."

His eyes scanned the area.

"Now, we need to find the lowest point," Zane said.

Opie looked at me just as I looked at him: "The cave," we said in unison.

"Is it dry?" Zane asked.

Opie and I nodded. "We found a fire ring inside," I said.

"Good, so we don't have to worry about it turning into an underground swimming hole on us. Opie, since you know where the cave is, I want you and Bo to take Randall there."

He nodded at me and Cash.

"While we help Randall onto Moonshine, I want you two boys," he said, "to gather those sleeping bags and water and whatever else you think we might need. Throw those sleeping bags over Checkers and rig up the water jugs so he can carry them. Now hurry!"

The wind was blowing horizontally now. The fire we had built was blazing hot—whipped to a frenzy by all the extra oxygen. Glowing embers somersaulted into the air and square-danced with each other.

I hunted for a catch rope to lash the water jugs together.

Then I unfurled the sleeping bags and threw them one by one onto Checkers' back. Cash helped me lift the water jugs. I knew Cash was weak from hunger but he did not quit. *A true Bulldogger*, I thought.

The rumble of thunder and the close cracks of lightning meant the storm was getting closer. I glanced up at the half daylight, half twilight sky. A sheet of water rained from the wall cloud. The tornado funnel danced a frightening jig over the power lines. As the lines sparked and sputtered, I couldn't help but wonder, *How in the world are we going to escape it?*

Opie and Bo were leading Randall off to the cave, when a bolt of lightning flashed like a strobe light. It spooked Checkers. I held tightly to his reins but there was no calming him. A horse's first defense to most anything is to flee. If I let go now, no doubt Checkers would be hightailing it across the prairie in a New York minute. No telling if I would ever see him again.

I gripped the reins tighter.

After all we had been through on this trip, I was not about to lose my horse, too.

Chapter 22
Trapped!

ZANE STRUGGLED to untie the tarp, but it was no use. The devilish wind ripped it from his hands time after time. Watching him, my first thought was that the tarp would make a good barrier between a cold, hard-rock cave floor and a sleeping bag. I was pretty sure that was Zane's thinking, too.

Piñon jays frenetically called to each other in a rhythmic *krawk-kraw-krawk*. And then a huge flock of them took flight, creating a bluish-gray cloud overhead. The wind determined their direction. I watched as the flock was swept first one way, and then another, back and forth across the sky until finally they were out of sight.

I tugged hard on Checkers' reins. Cash and I bent our heads against the wind. Dust and grit burned my eyes and nicked my skin. I pulled my bandanna up over my nose and mouth.

The sky had turned a wicked black by the time we made our way to the patch of buffalo grass. We had almost made it across when a herd of mule deer bounded across in front of us. Checkers reared and I lost hold of his reins. The water jugs fell off his back. He reared again, wild-eyed, and took off, running as fast as he could, back the way we had come. The sleeping bags floated off his back one by one into the air before landing in colorful heaps on the ground.

"Checkers!" I cried.

"Go! Go get him!" Cash yelled. "I can get these."

"You don't know how to find the cave," I hollered. "And there's no way you can carry all this by yourself . . ."

He was kind enough not to argue. I untied the catch rope from the water jugs, and we each grabbed a jug and a couple of the sleeping bags Checkers had left behind.

"This way," I said.

I led us to the top of the rise. We made our way down into the ravine. Moonshine was nowhere to be seen either. The wind whipped the vines over the cave entrance.

Inside, Randall sat leaning against a wall. He held a flashlight on Opie and Bo, who were busy building another tipi fire inside the old fire ring. I dropped the water jug and the sleeping bags.

"Checkers took off," I said. "I have to go find him."

Before anyone could stop me, I took off out of there. I sprinted up the rocky path and over the top edge. I ran down the slight hill. All the while I searched the landscape, looking for Checkers.

I saw him, or what I thought might have been him in a bramble thicket. I tore through it. No Checkers. I kept running. I had almost made it back to our original camp when a wave of wind nearly blew me over. I scanned the sky. Hail

the size of peas pelted me. I ignored that, too. I shielded my eyes with my hand to see better. No sign of Checkers. That's when the storm cloud burst. Rain fell in torrents. I was soaked before I could take a step but I kept running.

A rumble, like thunder, began, but instead of fading, it turned into a roar. It sounded like a train, only there were no train tracks anywhere nearby.

The combination of high winds and rain knocked me to the ground. The storm sucked my hat off my head. I reached for it, but it was already long gone. I tried to stand but the sheer force of the wind pinned me to the ground and then rolled me over and over. Grass, mud, and rain filled my mouth. I started to choke . . . and I thought about the stories of cows and houses plucked up and sent flying through the air in Oklahoma storms. My short life passed before my eyes.

It was almost over . . .

Chapter 23
Touchdown!

T HE HAND THAT TORE me away from the storm was strong and sure. I felt rather than saw it grab my arm and drag me across the muddy ground. Then it lifted me up. When the next bolt of lightning flashed, Zane's face became clear.

Before I could say a word, he tucked me back under his arm, like a football, and commenced running back to the cave. He ran as if a pack of three-hundred-pound-plus Sooner football linesmen was after him. He made good time for an old cowboy.

When he hit the ravine, he gripped me tighter and plunged over the lip. He half slid down the path to the cave. Just as we made it to the entrance, but before you could say "touchdown," lightning struck again.

This time the bolt split that big dead cottonwood tree.

One half of the tree went one way; one half, went ours.

Zane ducked, made one last desperate leap, and pushed me inside ahead of him deeper into the cave, right before the tree crashed to the ground, blocking the entrance and any chance for us to get out.

Chapter 24

The Mysterious Man with Two Names

WHAT I HAVE COME to know about caves since that stormy night we spent huddled together in sleeping bags around that fire has kept me awake many a night since. Learning that mountain lions, raccoons, and both rattlesnake and copperheads enter caves to eat either mice or bats would be unsettling for the toughest bulldogger, I'd like to think.

And yes, there were bats—hundreds of them, hanging here and there in clusters from the ceiling and filling nooks and crannies in the walls. Come to find out wild animals also use caves as shelter from storms, just like the one we were riding out now. Needless to say, none of us slept more than a few winks that night.

Me, I couldn't get over what might have happened to me had Zane not come after me. And every time I thought about Checkers, a lump formed in my throat.

Despite its drawbacks, it was impossible not to be grateful for the cave—given the storm raging outside. But knowing we were trapped inside threw all of us Bulldoggers into a bit of a panic, until Randall and Zane reminded us that there was not a single thing we could do about it.

"After all," Randall said, "we are safe from the storm."

As far as the livestock and horses went, Zane assured us it was in their nature to run from such acts of nature, and with any luck, they had escaped its wrath.

I, for one, appreciated how Zane and Randall stayed so calm and matter-of-fact. It gave me confidence that somehow we would get out of here and home in one piece. Our trip to Pueblo might have been ruined, but there's nothing like a tornado to make you realize what's important in life. For now, there was nothing left for us to do but rest up from all the excitement and tackle the problem with fresh eyes, in the morning.

Randall said he had just the thing to take our minds off the thunder storm raging outside: a story about buried treasure. We grabbed our sleeping bags and scooted a little closer to the fire.

"Folks talk about the Man with Two Names," Randall said, clearing his throat and setting his hat aside. "He's buried in an unmarked grave, all by his lonesome, up on that hillside."

"We saw the grave," Opie said.

"It was that pile of rocks, right?" I said.

"You boys are very observant," Randall said.

The campfire threw distorted shadows of us against the cave walls. The bread, pickles, and piñon nuts had made for a light supper, but we would not have had the nuts at all if not for Cash. Before all the ruckus started, he had found Bo's bandanna on the ground, the nuts still inside. Bo must have dropped it. Cash had stuffed it in his pocket and promptly forgotten about it until his stomach growled. Thanks to him, we had a little snack to go with our ghost story.

"It started early one morning back in 1896," Randall said, lowering his voice to a menacing whisper. "A gunshot broke the stillness of what used to be a small town over near the Salt Fork River. A town named Mesa."

"It's more like a spot on the road than a town, now," Zane said. "All that's left are crumbling foundations and one historical marker where the old courthouse used to sit."

"Ah, the courthouse," Randall said, and sighed. "The source of many a man's sorrow. But I am getting ahead of myself. As I said, it started with a gunshot, early one crisp fall morning. A few townsmen went to investigate, and discovered Harry Davis, the owner of the local roadhouse, had been shot dead.

"No one could understand why anyone would shoot Harry because he was that rare model citizen in an otherwise lawless town. While the drovers—the men who drove the herds—would get liquored up and fight duels in the streets over prideful hurts, Harry was more likely to be found performing some act of kindness for his neighbors. If a cowboy got out of hand, Harry was the one quick to step in and resolve the situation. If a man needed a meal, Harry fed him. No questions asked."

"Why would anyone kill such a man?" Cash said.

"Exactly," Randall said. "So you can understand the confusion when, in December, a public sale was announced of the dead man's holdings, which included thirty horses, five steers, and some valuable town lots. Come to find out county records indicated Harry wasn't the dead man's real name. A

115

probate case was filed a few years later by a Mr. Bruce Lance in the case of a Mr. Clement Lance, alias Harry Davis."

"What's 'probate' mean?" I asked, stifling a sleepy yawn.

"That would be when someone brings to court the last will and testament of a person to prove it is the genuine article."

"Why do you think he had two names?" Opie asked.

"Some people said his death was linked to a mysterious arson fire that destroyed the county courthouse a few months earlier. That case resulted in a grand jury investigation, but no charges were ever brought against anyone. Other people said he got on the wrong side of a horse trade."

We all perked up at that.

"But I'm going to tell you what really happened." Randall paused. He leaned in closer. We leaned in closer, too. He took a deep breath and released a long, slow breath. When next he spoke, he whispered low, "And do not ask how I know."

One by one, he looked each of us square in the eyes.

"It seems thirty odd years before, Harry Davis ran with some rough characters, namely the William Coe gang.

"William Coe, or Captain Bill as he was known, was rumored to have fought with the Confederates during the Civil War, hence the military title. He was a Southern boy who had worked as a carpenter and a stone mason before settling in No Man's Land. His gang fluctuated between thirty to fifty outlaws. Their crime of choice was rustling cattle—but they weren't adverse to taking horses, sheep, or mules.

"Coe built a fortress high up on a ridge to protect himself and his gang. It had thick walls—some three feet deep, gun portholes rather than windows, and living quarters for all his men. He even had a blacksmith shop built; it came in handy when they needed to change the brands on the stolen livestock before shipping it out to the markets in Missouri and Kansas. His hideaway became known as Robbers' Roost.

"The dirty deeds of the Coe gang went on for years. They raided ranches and military installations from Fort Union, New Mexico, to the south; Taos, New Mexico, to the west; and as far north as Denver, Colorado. They also held up freight caravans traveling along the Santa Fe Trail. Then one day they went too far. They raided a large sheep ranch and murdered two men. They stole the sheep, left the bodies behind, and took off for Pueblo, Colorado.

"That's where we were headed," Bo said.

"Yes, it is," Randall said. "The crimes landed them on the Most Wanted list. Soldiers from Fort Collins came after them, and one fateful day, the army attacked Robbers' Roost with a canon. The three-foot-thick rock walls crumbled. Several of the outlaws were killed. Coe and a few others escaped, but the ones who were caught were hanged on the spot.

"Coe eluded capture for about a year until one night, while sleeping in the bunkhouse of a lady friend, the woman's fourteen-year-old son slipped away and alerted soldiers at the nearby fort to his whereabouts."

"That boy was a hero!" Cash said.

"That took a lot of courage," Opie said.

We all agreed with a nod of our heads.

Randall continued. "Coe was arrested that night. However, before he could be brought to trial, vigilantes took matters into their own hands and hung him from a cottonwood tree while he was still handcuffed and shackled. Opie, what did you call that earlier in the truck?"

"That would be a *cottonwood blossom*."

"Right. Anyway, the next day, Coe's body was discovered

hanging from the tree. They buried him right where they found him."

"So, the Man with Two Names was actually Captain Bill Coe?" Bo said.

"Not quite. Remember I said some outlaws escaped."

"Ohhh," Bo said.

"Well, I have it on good authority that the Man with Two Names was one of those who escaped. He lived in parts unknown for nearly twenty years. He built a life for himself as a roadhouse manager, with a new wife and a son. When his wife died of consumption, Clement Lance, alias Harry Davis, returned to No Man's Land. Racked with guilt, he opened the roadhouse where he spent the rest of his days helping others, trying to make amends for his crimes.

"In fact, the morning he was shot he was on his way to help a young mother who had just lost her husband in a freak accident.

"When he was shot, Clement had a shovel and a map in his saddle bag. On closer inspection afterwards it turned out the map clearly indicated buried treasure. Some believed it was Captain Bill's loot that for many years has been thought to be buried in a place called Flag Springs Arroyo.

"No one has ever discovered the exact location, but folks here always talk about hearing and seeing strange sights when they pass by that lonesome grave."

"What kind of strange things?" Cash asked.

"They say some hear a mournful cry, while others tell of a digging noise, the sound of someone turning dirt with a shovel, over and over."

"That's creepy," Bo said, with a visible shiver.

"We got chills when we passed by there earlier," I said, and pulled my sleeping bag closer around me.

"Why do you think they buried him way out here?" Opie asked in a tight little voice.

"It's hard to say exactly," Randall said, "but it was probably easier to bury him where he died than to haul him to the nearest graveyard, which would have been some miles away. And maybe they took into account the benefits of burying him in higher ground, given that a volatile river prone to flooding makes a bad place for a cemetery. I've heard tales of graves being washed away and caskets being found sticking out of the mud. The last thing anybody wants is the body of a dead outlaw floating into town."

"Maybe the Man with Two Names is trying to tell us where the loot is hidden," I said.

"Maybe it is hidden in this cave!" Cash said.

"This is no arroyo," Opie observed.

"True," I said, "but that reminds me—Bo found something kind of interesting in that arroyo we drove into, accidentally."

"What did you find, son?" Zane asked, turning to Bo.

"I guess when the flood water washed out the road, it uncovered a boneyard," Bo said.

"Giant bones," I said. "Bigger than I've ever seen."

"Actually, I'm not surprised," Randall said. "They've discovered quite a few dinosaur bones in this area."

"Told you," Bo said, and bumped my shoulder with his.

"You did say they looked prehistoric," I said.

"If they turn out to be a complete skeleton, you will be a rich man," Randall said. "I remember reading that a skeleton of a mature *Tyrannosaurus rex* went for more than $8 million in a New York auction, and that was back in 1998."

"Wow!" Bo said, sitting up a little straighter.

"Now hold on a minute, son," Zane said. "First, this is

Fender property. Anything you found on it belongs to Randall's family and rightly so."

"But it is Bo's discovery," Randall said. "Finders keepers."

"That's mighty generous of you," Zane said, "but let's also remember if it does turn out to be such a find, that's the kind of fossil discovery that can improve the world's collective knowledge if it can get into the hands of the right scientist."

"Good point," Randall said.

"So let's wait and see how we all feel in the morning," Zane said. "Maybe it'll be something, maybe it'll be nothing. What I do know is we all should try to get some shut-eye now. Who knows what tomorrow will bring—so far every day on this trip has been more exciting than the last."

"Agreed," Randall said. "It has been one long, eventful day."

"I hate to think what other damage we may find that twister has done," Zane said.

I couldn't help but notice, as I lay down to sleep, that nobody had said anything about one other important detail: *Even if a search party was looking for us, how would anyone know to look for us in a cave?*

Chapter 25
The Bowels of the Earth

ME AND CHECKERS WERE together again, only this time we were galloping down a dirt road. A sense of urgency drove me to spur him to go faster as if we were being chased. But when I looked behind us no one was there.

I awoke with a start. I opened my eyes and for a moment I thought I had gone blind during the night—thankfully before I could panic my eyes adjusted to the dark. The squeaks of bats peppered the quiet of the cave and the acrid smell of the campfire made my nose twitch.

I felt around for my flashlight, and then realized I had kicked it to the bottom of my sleeping bag. I could feel it with my toes. I dug it out and switched it on, but the beam faded in and out. *Darn*, I thought, *the battery is nearly dead*. And then it went out altogether.

My stomach growled. *Man, I'm hungry*. I thought about

the big breakfast my mother had made us before we left, Friday morning, and what I knew she'd be making for my brother given that it was Sunday morning: Bacon. Eggs. Blueberry muffins. Fried potatoes. My mouth watered at the thought of it—and the thought of my mother brought tears to my eyes.

Deciding it was better not to wake Randall, Zane, or the other Bulldoggers as no telling what time it was, I tried to be quiet. It wasn't easy. I couldn't see my hand in front of my face, much less read the face of a watch. *How much longer will we be trapped in this cave*, I wondered. I didn't like the answer that popped into my head.

I shivered and crawled back into my sleeping bag. My bag felt damp and cold, but I knew if I made a cocoon, my warm breath would slowly warm up the space inside. I closed my eyes and tried to go back to sleep. No such luck, too many thoughts trailed through my mind to allow sleep to take over, though I must admit the thought that dominated all the others had to do with being trapped in a cave. *Maybe I'm a little claustrophobic*, I thought. That thought made me sit up again.

"We have to find a way out!"

"Don't worry, Dru, we'll get out of here," Zane said.

"Oops, sorry Zane. I didn't mean to say that aloud. Sorry if I woke you."

"You didn't wake me. I've been laying here thinking."

"Me, too," Bo said.

I chuckled. "You, too, Bo! Funny, I thought I was the only one awake."

"Me, too," Bo said.

"Well you're not, neither one of you, so get over yourselves," Cash said. "Opie and I are both awake, and so is Randall."

That pronouncement brought a round of laughter, which I couldn't help but think boded well for the day.

"Well, as long as we're all up," Opie said, "Maybe, together, we could move that tree."

"That's what I was thinking," Zane said. "It's worth at least a try."

"Does anybody have a flashlight that works?" I asked.

"Here you go," Randall said. I felt something land on my sleeping bag.

"Mine still works, too," Opie said.

With a bit of light available now, we were able to stand without treading on each other.

"Could you shine it over here," Zane said.

Opie and I pointed our beams where Zane's voice had come from, which ended up being the front of the cave. The giant downed cottonwood tree covered the entire entrance, like a wall.

"That is one huge tree," I said.

"And it's no lightweight, either," Opie noted.

"Seeing it now, I realize we're lucky someone wasn't killed when it fell," Zane said. "Okay now, let's give it a go."

Together, we lined up with our shoulders against the tree trunk. "On the count of three," Zane said. "One. Two. Three."

We all pushed as hard as we could. The tree didn't budge.

"It's not only heavy, but I believe it's wedged in the opening," Zane said. His voice sounded the most defeated I'd heard it since our streak of bad luck had begun two days ago.

Ever the optimist, Opie said, "Maybe there's another way out."

I found myself wanting to believe him. "Maybe, we didn't explore very far last time."

"There was no need to find another way out, before now," Opie said.

"And now," I said, "we have no other choice."

"Now hold up there guys, let's talk about this for a minute," Zane said. "Get back in your sleeping bags. Might as well turn off those flashlights to save the batteries, too, while we weigh the pros and cons of Opie's suggestion."

We all slipped back inside our bags and waited in the dark. Randall's voice broke the dark and silence first.

"To start with," he said, "what are our choices?"

"The way I see it," Zane answered, "we have three choices: One, we can use our pocketknives to whittle a hole through that enormous tree trunk—should only take a year or two. Two, we can sit here and hope someone finds us—that might actually take a lot longer than the whittling. Three, we can look for another way out."

"Well, I do hate to think what they would find if we wait . . ." Randall said.

"I agree," Zane said. "Strike option two."

"As for cutting through that tree with a pocketknife, I think your time estimate is pretty accurate, Zane. It would be like trying to empty the Atlantic Ocean with a tablespoon."

With that, the cave went quiet.

"I propose," I said, "that the four of us Bulldoggers search for another opening in the cave."

"I agree," Opie said. "We are a lot smaller, so we'll fit through smaller crevices. None of us are injured, either. And, if we use the buddy system, we should be plenty safe."

"Now wait a minute," Randall said. "We appreciate your willingness to do this, however, it is never wise to go deeper into a cave without proper equipment and experience, neither of which you boys have."

"We have ropes and flashlights," Bo said.

"And leather gloves," Cash said.

"We have our catch ropes," I added.

"What happens when the flashlights die leaving you in the bowels of the earth with no light and no way out?"

"We have no way out right now," I said, almost in a whisper. (I did not want to come off as a smart mouth.)

Before Randall or Zane could reprimand me, Opie spoke up. "What if we tie the ropes together, end to end, and use them as a guide to find our way back," Opie said, "kinda like leaving bread crumbs but this will work even in the dark."

"We could go as far as the ropes will reach and see if there is another way out," I said. "And if our flashlights die, we'll be able to feel our way back, using the ropes."

"That's not a bad plan," Randall said. "However, you boys need to understand there are real dangers inherent to caves. You could fall. If you fall you could break bones or crack your head open. Those rocks do not budge. Unless they are loose. That's actually another danger, falling rocks.

"Bats carry rabies," he added. "And bat poop, or guano, can carry viruses. Bottom line is steer clear of bats and what they leave behind."

"We'll use our bandannas," Cash said, "to cover our noses and mouths. Right, guys?"

"I have mine," I said.

"Me, too," Bo said.

"Awww. I can't find mine," Opie said. "That was my lucky bandanna, too."

"You can use mine," Randall said. "I'm sure yours will turn up."

"Last but not least," Zane said, "a reminder. If you happen to find it, don't drink the water."

125

"No argument there," Cash piped up. We all laughed.

"I know you're laughing *with* me not at me," Cash quipped, which made us all laugh even harder.

The joking took some of the tension out of the room. But when Zane spoke again, I could tell he wanted to make sure we knew that exploring a cave under these conditions was no laughing matter.

"Remember," he said, "you may find crawling is your best option once the cave narrows. And finding water, so long as you don't drink it, could be good. It has to get in somehow. It might mean there is another opening somewhere."

"Or not," Randall said. "It could be seeping in. By the way, have you noticed a slight breeze in here?"

"It made the flames of the fire dance, last night," Opie said.

"Great—that gives me more hope as far as you boys finding another opening. Now the size of what that opening might be is anybody's guess," Randall said.

"Okay, I guess that just about does it," Zane said. "Gather your gear and wits about you, and let's get you spelunking."

I turned on my flashlight, and we stood. Bo, Cash, Opie, and I piled all the ropes we could find in a mound and started tying them together end to end. With four thirty-five-foot-long lariats knotted together to form one long rope, we figured we'd have close to a hundred and twenty feet of rope. Zane tied one end to the heaviest water jug to anchor it. We rolled up the rest, put on our work gloves, and pointed our flashlight, as Randall called it, "into the bowels of the earth."

We decided we would take turns carrying the coil of rope. Bo volunteered to go first. He and Cash paired up. Opie and I took the front.

"Remember, there's a drop-off right away," Opie said.

He pointed his light down into the pit. I leaned down,

steadied myself with a hand on the floor, and jumped. The pit was as deep as I was tall. I reached up and helped Opie down. Since he had already done it before, he seemed to know what to expect. Cash went next. Bo unrolled some of the coiled rope then handed the coil down to me, then he jumped in too. Opie and Cash cast their lights about the pit.

The cave walls seemed to be solid rock and for a moment I had a sinking feeling: if this was as far as the cave went, we're back to square one. I refused to accept the possibility of that. I felt my way around the perimeter of the space, one hand over the other as I walked my hands along the wall. When I had gone almost all the way around, I touched nothingness.

"Need some light here," I hollered.

Opie and Cash trained their beams on me.

"Hmmm, looks like a narrow crevice," I said. "It's going to be a tight fit, but let's give it a go."

Being the smallest, Opie went first. He turned his slender body sideways, and kept the beam from his flashlight focused on the cave floor. I followed him into the slim passageway.

"Going down," Opie said.

"Going down," I repeated.

"Going down," Cash said to warn Bo.

The cave floor sloped downward for about ten feet, I figured. It pitched to the right, and then to the left. "It will be difficult to judge how far we are going when we're stepping sideways," I said.

"And it is very slow going," Opie said.

The floor did level off, but the passageway grew more and more narrow. "Bo," I said, "your dad never would have made it through here."

"I know," Bo said, "I'm barely squeezing through."

"Listen," I said. "Hear that?"

127

"Sounds like a waterfall," Opie said.

"Can you see an end to this canyon," I said.

"Nope," Opie said. "It keeps twisting and turning."

"I wonder how far away that waterfall is," I said.

"No telling," Opie said. "The acoustics magnify the sound."

"It could be quite a ways," Bo said. "We have leveled off somewhat, but we are still going downhill."

"It feels pretty chilly in here," I said.

"A constant fifty-eight degrees," Opie said.

"Felt colder last night," Cash said.

"We've traveled about twenty feet is my guess," Bo said.

"You want me to carry that rope?" Cash said.

"Sure, mighty nice of you to offer."

"No problem."

"Hold up, Opie," I said. "Bo and Cash are switching off."

Bo passed the rope to Opie. He handed Bo the flashlight. "We aren't going to be able to switch places," Bo said.

"Too tight a squeeze," Cash said.

"Dru," Bo said, "we're ready."

We inched forward again.

"Oh man," Opie said. "Watch your step." He no more said that than I stepped into water. "From the sound of that splash, the water's getting deeper."

"That means it's flowing this way," I said. "There must be another opening somewhere up ahead."

I took a few more steps and found myself up to my knees in water. "Brrrr, that's cold!" A mineral smell assaulted my nose. "Smelly, too!"

The narrow canyon grew wider with each step forward. Water sloshed in my boots. Suddenly the space opened into a cistern-shaped room. The four of us stood shoulder to shoulder now.

"The waterfall has got to be in here somewhere," Bo said.

"It sounds like it is over there, to the right," I said.

Opie shone his beam in that direction. "There! I see it. I see where the water is coming in."

"I see it too!" Cash said.

"It's a pretty decent size opening up there," Bo said.

"I'm surprised how little water is actually flowing in. It sounded like a spigot filling a bathtub, but it's only a trickle," Opie observed.

"That could be good or bad for us," I said. "It may be a trickle because it's a small opening."

"Possibly too small for us to wiggle through," Bo said.

"Only one way to find out," I said.

"Cash," Bo said, "how much rope do you have left?"

Cash held up the coil. "This much."

"Where's the rest of it?" I asked.

Cash picked up the rope and held it high. "Uh oh," he said.

"That does not sound good," Bo said.

"Uh, fellas, I have some bad news," Cash said. "I'm afraid, this is all there is. The rope must have come untied."

"That's impossible," Opie said. "Didn't everyone use a Double Fisherman's to join their ropes?"

Silence. "Anybody?" Opie asked.

"I think I used a square knot," Bo said.

"Me, too," I said.

"Me, three," Cash said. "It's the only one I know by heart that you can use to join two things together."

We all turned to Opie. The look on his face was priceless. Unspeakable, but priceless.

"We're doomed," Cash cried.

Chapter 26
Dead Batteries

O NCE WE CLAWED Cash off the proverbial ceiling, we assured him that so long as we did not panic we were not, as he put it, "doomed."

"Have you learned nothing from watching Zane and Randall these past two days, Cash?" I asked. "You can work yourself out of almost any situation so long as you don't panic. Now somebody, shine your flashlight back and up that way at the ceiling for me."

"Sorry, can't. Mine just quit," Bo said.

"My batteries are running low, and I don't know what you think you'll see, but here you go," Opie said, and with that he turned on his flashlight.

The cave glowed in gold and ambers. It looked like something out of the movie *Journey to the Center of the Earth*.

"Wow!" Cash said, "Are those stalactites or stalagmites hanging from the ceiling? They're huge!"

"Stalactites grow down," Opie said. "Stalagmites grow up from the cave floor. This cave has a lot more formations, or *speleothems*, than that. What kind depends on whether the water drips, seeps, condenses, flows, or ponds.

"Speaking of ponds, there could be a drop off under here," Opie warned.

"Thanks," I said. "Good to know."

"Maybe just one of us should walk across there."

"I'll go," I said.

"Tie the rope around your waist, Dru," Bo said. "Just in case the cave floor drops off. We'll hold onto this end, so we can pull you out if need be."

I looped the lariat around my waist and snugged it up. I took a step, then another, and another. A few more and I had made it across.

"It's solid," I said. "Come on."

As Bo, Cash, and Opie waded through the water, a trickle of water high up on the sloping wall caught my eye.

"Could you point your flashlight up there Opie," I asked. "I need to get a better look . . . Thanks, that helps. Hmmm, it looks slippery, but I think I see handholds. Don't you?"

"I think you're right," Opie said.

"It could be worse," Bo said.

"I like your attitude," I said.

"I'm glad it's not worse," Cash said. "Have a little fear of heights, I do."

With that I stepped up onto the ledge and began inching my way, one handhold at a time. The ledge did not go straight up but rather wound around to the right and to the left and back again. I came to a level spot and waited for the others to catch up.

Opie, who was behind me, held the only light. He stood

beside me shining it so the others could see where to put their feet and hands.

"Oooo," Bo said. "Who did that?"

"What?" I said. "Oh, for Pete's sake. That stinks."

"Wasn't me," Cash said.

"At least there's a little breeze," I said.

Opie shone his light down at our feet.

"What's that?" Cash asked.

"Bat guano," Opie said. "Tons of it."

"No wonder it stinks," I said.

Opie moved the light to the wall.

"There they are. A whole colony of bats." The bats were huddled together and seemed to be asleep; the light from the flashlight didn't bother them at all. "They sleep during the day and go out at dusk to hunt for bugs to eat," Opie said.

"Are those vampire bats?" Cash asked, and I could hear the trepidation in his voice.

"Not sure," Opie said. "It's so dark in here I can't see them very well. They might be big-eared bats. I've heard they frequent Oklahoma caves."

"Pull your bandannas up now everybody," I said. "Remember what Randall and Zane said about inhaling this stuff."

Opie shone the light down again. "That pile of guano has stuff crawling in it," he said.

"It looks like the whole pile is moving," I said.

"Gross," Cash said, his voice muffled behind his bandanna.

"Watch your step," I said.

Opie made sure everyone could see as we navigated the tight path around the nasty pile of guano.

"This way," I said.

We continued following the stream through what had now become squishy, slippery mud. We ended up at a place where water flowed down the cave walls.

I looked up, reached as far above my head as I could, and found an outcropping of rock.

"I think we're . . ." but before I could finish my sentence the cave went black.

Chapter 27
Freedom!

"WE ARE GOING to die," Cash screamed.
"Not if I can help it," I said.
"Or me," Bo said.

"Or me," Opie said, louder than the rest of us.

All of our flashlights were now dead. In the dark, with our voices all muffled from the bandannas, I felt as if I was in some strange nightmare.

"The water flowed from up here somewhere," I said. "I'm going to go as far as I can climb."

"How will you see where to go?" Cash asked.

"I'll have to see with my hands and feet. I'm going to take off my boots so I can hold on better."

"Be careful, Dru," Bo said. "I don't want to be running an ad for a new best friend when we get home."

That drew chuckles all round. Once I had toed off my cowboy boots, I moved my left hand back and forth across the bedrock above my head until I found a place to grab on. I pulled myself up and put my toe on the place where my hand had been. Up, up I went, one handhold, one toehold at a time. Time seemed to stand still. I barely breathed as I made my way, like a tarantula, up the face of the cave. *The Amazing Spider-Man has nothing on me*, I thought.

Eventually, I came to a much larger outcropping of rock, big enough I thought to stand on. I gripped it with both hands and hoisted myself up and landed on my belly. I pulled my legs up and over. Got my feet under me and stood, with great care, clinging to whatever I could find to hold onto.

I dared to look up, straight up. I could not believe what I saw. In place of the thick darkness was a bright light coming through a hole in the ceiling.

"I see daylight!" I hollered. "I can see blue sky and white fluffy clouds!"

I heard cheering from below. Freedom felt so close, I almost forgot I was still basically trapped underground. I couldn't see any detail in the wall to which I clung. I gritted my teeth, determined to not only get myself out of this mess, but the others, as well. *I still have the rope wrapped around me*, I thought. *Things could be worse.*

Desperate to find another crack in the rock for my next handhold, I reached as high as I could, searching the wall with my fingertips. I found one. And another. *Yes! I'm making it. Almost to the top.* Through the hole in the ceiling above me I could see the tips of buffalo grass blowing in the wind.

My head poked up and out. One arm, and then the other. I clawed at the grass and grabbed hold of two handfuls, enough to pull my shoulders up past the opening in the ground.

My arms shook with fatigue as I lifted myself up and out.

135

I sat on the edge and sighed deeply, breathing in the fresh, warm air. "I'm out!" I hollered down to my friends.

Joyful cheers floated up from below.

I clambered to my feet and let the sun beat warm me for a moment. I had no clue what time it was, but the sun was way up. *How long were we down there, anyway? Now, if I could find something to anchor this rope to,* I thought, *I could help the other guys get out easier.* I scanned the landscape. Nothing but buffalo grass as far as the eye could see.

Then, I blinked. Was I dreaming or, maybe, hallucinating from too many guano fumes because I could swear I saw a cowgirl on a horse!

I blinked several times and looked again. Up high on the ridge, yes, it was a cowgirl, waving her hat in the air. I watched her kick-start her horse and ride down the hill toward me hollering, hollering words I could not understand until she got closer. And then I saw a riderless horse following her across the land: Checkers!

"Where did you come from," the cowgirl asked. "I've been looking for you! We all have!" She jumped off her horse. She looked to be about my age.

"The others are still down there," I said.

"Down where?" She looked all around and then stared at me as if I was crazy.

"Down this shaft." I showed her the opening in the ground. By now, Checkers had arrived. He gave me a good sniff as if to confirm it was me. When he seemed satisfied, I gave him a big hug. "I'm so glad to see you, Checkers."

"How did you find him?" I asked the girl.

"Actually, he found me. Showed up and started following me and Kenworth, there." She pointed to her big chestnut gelding.

"What do you mean he just started following you?" Far as I knew, I was the only one Checkers followed, and mainly at mealtime.

She shrugged. "Some folks say I have a way with horses."

I didn't know what she meant by that, but it was clear Checkers liked her.

"My dad is a ranch hand for the Fenders," she said. "Heard you all went missing. We would have started looking for you sooner, but when the tornado sirens went off, we had to go to the fraidy hole. Once the weather cleared out, my dad took off searching for you; he was out most of the night but no luck. Soon as it was light out today, me and Kenworth joined the search party. Dad had found the wreck site last night, so that's where I started. I found what was left of your camp. Basically, one fence panel is still standing, and another one is wrapped around a tree."

I was starting to feel like I'd been a little rude about Checkers' wandering affections. Obviously, this cowgirl had been trying to help. And she had reunited me with my horse.

"That was darn nice of you all to look for us," I said, "and thank you for finding Checkers, but we still need to get the others out from below—the sooner, the better."

The girl but nodded in agreement.

"Now I've been trying to figure out how best to do that," I said. "If I could borrow your lasso, I think I can knot it to mine, loop one end of the lasso over your saddle horn, and then toss the other end down to my friends—they're the ones down in the hole there—so they have something to help them climb out."

"Sounds like a plan," she said.

I knotted the two ropes together—this time using the right knot. *No more knots coming untied on my watch*, I thought.

137

"Do you have anything heavy I could use to tie onto the rope, to weight the end, to make sure it makes it all the way to where the guys are? That shaft curves about midway down."

"I have a full water bottle with a loop attached to the lid."

"Perfect," I said.

When all was ready, I knelt by the hole and hollered, "Hey guys! Can you hear me?"

"Yeah!" Their voices were muffled.

"Where'd you go?" Bo hollered. "We thought something had happened to you!"

"Sorry—had to get some help. I'm throwing you a rope now. Watch out below!" I lowered the water bottle into the hole and let its weight pull the rope through my hands. After a few moments, I felt a tug on the rope.

"Got it!" Bo yelled.

"Holler when ready!" I yelled. "I have help up here!"

"What?"

"I'm going to pull you up!"

"How?"

The explanation would not translate, so I shouted, "Checkers!"

"Okay!" Bo yelled.

I signaled to the girl with a nod. She backed Kenworth, step by step. The rope started moving. She kept a steady tension on it.

"How many are down there?

"Three."

"Any adults?"

"Not right here. As far as I know, Zane and Randall are still trapped in the main cave."

I kept watching the hole for someone to appear at the end of the rope.

"I see the top of a head," I yelled. "It's Cash!"

Cash looked up then. "I see you," he said.

The lasso loop was around his waist, and he held onto the rope and walked his feet up the side. When he neared the top, I reached down, grabbed his hand, and helped him up over the rim.

He pulled his bandanna down, blinked, and squinted to adjust his eyes—the sunshine was blinding after being in the dark so long. I hugged him, and he hugged me back.

I loosened the rope and slipped it over his head. The water bottle still attached, I lowered the rope once more.

"Head's up!" I hollered. The next thing I heard was another "Ready," coming from below.

Cash knelt and peered into the shaft with me. Pretty soon I saw the top of Opie's blond head come into view.

"Opie!" We both yelled.

"Hey!" He hollered back. As he drew closer, thanks to the help of Kenworth and the girl, I realized, suddenly, that I had never asked her name.

Cash and I each took hold of one of Opie's hands and pulled until he was safely back on terra firma. It was hugs and slaps on the back all around, again.

I sent the water bottle down the tube once more. It was time to bring up my best friend. "Head's up, Bo!" I hollered.

Bo gave the sign that he was ready, and the three of us knelt by the opening, watching for his head to pop up.

"There he is!" Cash yelled.

Bo looked up and gave us a little wave and a grin. "Long time, no see," he yelled.

We laughed at his little joke like silly-nillies. "Brought you something," Bo said, as we helped him over the rim. My boots were tucked into the rope. He removed them and handed them to me. "You owe me big time. Those boots smell like something died in them."

Laughing, the four of us hugged and fist-bumped and back slapped, and hugged some more.

"Now that we are all safely out of that rat hole," I said, turning to face our rescuer, "let me say I've never been as glad to see somebody in my whole life, miss. I'm Dru Winterhalter, and these are my buddies. That's Opie George."

"Pleased to meet you and thank you," Opie said. He started to reach out to shake hands, but pulled back. "Excuse my manners, but I'm filthy."

"And this is Bo Gillock," I said.

Bo nodded, hello. "Thank you doesn't seem adequate for what you've done here," Bo said, "but thank you."

"And this here is Cash Bennett," I said.

Cash smiled. "I'm very grateful to you, miss," Cash said.

"Nice to meet you all," the cowgirl said. "I'm Big Little Thunder Lavigne, but most folks call me BLT for short."

"It's great to meet you, and thanks again, but as much as I'd like to chitchat," I said, "Randall and Zane don't know if we're alive or dead, and it's been some time since we set out."

"Yeah," Bo said. "I'm sure they're worried about us, and wouldn't mind getting out of that cave, either. If they hadn't thought it was looking like it might be our new permanent address, they would never have let us go alone in search of another opening."

"BLT," I said. "I'm not sure where we are. Do you know what cave we're talking about?"

"I do," she said.

"Well that's good news," I said. "Bad news is lightning struck that huge cottonwood tree by the entrance last night in the storm."

"It fell and trapped us inside the cave," Bo said.

"That was one doozy of a storm," BLT said. "By the way, I found this bandanna over there, snagged on a piñon tree. Would it maybe belong to any of you?"

"That's my lucky bandanna!" Opie said. "Moonshine was wearing it the day I found him at the horse auction. It proved lucky for him because any horse that wasn't sold that day was headed to the slaughterhouse."

"Seems it is still lucky," BLT said. "So, that's your gray I saw wandering on my way here? Well, he's fine, too. And I counted sixteen calves wandering loose to the north."

"Zane and Randall will be glad to hear that," Opie said.

I noticed something had caught BLT's eye.

"There's my dad's truck," she said, waving her hat in the air. Her dad must have seen her because he turned his red dually pickup in our direction.

"Now it's my turn to apologize," BLT said. "Excuse my manners. You guys must be starving."

Our eyes bugged out when we saw what she had in her saddlebag. She passed out bottles of water and bags of trail mix to each of us. By then, her dad had pulled up and hopped out of the truck. "Aren't you boys a sight for sore eyes!"

"Thank you, sir, for looking for us," I said. "I'm Dru— that's Bo, Cash, and Opie."

"Howdy, and, please, just call me Jon," he said. "So how did you boys end up here in the middle of this field?"

I exchanged a look with Bo. "Well," I said, "we took cover from the tornado in a cave."

"Then lightning struck a big dead cottonwood and it fell in front of the entrance," Bo said.

"It got wedged in so tight it wouldn't move—even with six of us trying," Cash said.

"Then, we decided to look for another way out of the cave," Opie said.

"And we found it," I said. "Right here." We showed him the vent hole.

"Golly Neds! You boys have had one heck of an adventure," he said, "but where are the adults that were with you? You were traveling with Randall Fender, right?"

"Yes, sir. He's still trapped in the cave with Bo's dad."

"We need to remedy that," he said.

"Mr. Fender's ankle may be broken," I said.

"All right. Here's what we'll do," he said. "I'm going to radio Colton and have him bring some harnesses. Whose horse is that?" He nodded at Checkers.

"Mine," I said.

"BLT, why don't you and Dru ride over to the cave to let Randall know everyone is safe and help is on the way. You three boys come along with me. We'll wait by the road for Colton to bring the harnesses for the two horses. I don't know how else to move that tree, other than to take a chain saw to it, but that would take more time than we've got."

"Okay, Dad," BLT said.

I tucked in my shirt and shoved my water bottle and bag of trail mix down inside. Bo gave me a knee up onto Checkers' back, and then he and the other Bulldoggers piled into Jon's truck. They took off in one direction while BLT and I headed for the cave. As it turned out, the hole we had emerged from emptied into land that lay atop the cave, and Randall had been right, the cave was massive. We hiked about an eighth of a mile to the main entrance, but it was a round-about path.

"It's funny," BLT said. "I've been all over this area many a time, and I've never noticed that hole in the ground."

"It's a wonder a steer hasn't broken a leg in it," I said.

At the top of the ravine, we tied the horses to a tree and scrambled down to the cave.

Seeing the fallen tree from the outside, I said, "Wow, it's a miracle we weren't killed." The tree trunk was split and dead wood lay everywhere.

"Hello! You guys in there?" I shouted. "It's Dru!"

"You're alive! Are the other Bulldoggers okay?" Randall asked.

"Yes, we're all fine!"

"So happy to hear your voice!" Zane said.

"Help is on the way!"

"Music to our ears!" Randall said.

While we waited for the rest of the fellas, I ate my trail mix. It was gone much too fast. "I don't think trail mix has ever tasted so darn good," I said, turning the bag upside down to shake out the very last crumb.

"It was my mom's idea to bring it along. She figured if I found you, you'd be hungry."

"She was right about that," I said.

"They're here," she said.

Chapter 28
Help Is on the Way!

"**THEY'RE HERE!**" I shouted, loud enough for Randall and Zane to hear me. BLT and I met the cavalry at the top of the ravine.

"Colton," Jon said, "this is Dru. He's the one who first popped up in the middle of the field, in that hole I showed you."

"Scotty has told me about you and the Bulldoggers Club," Colton said. "So, you're the hero of the day."

Cash, Opie, and Bo walked up beside me just in time to overhear Colton's words. "Oh, no!" I said, quickly. "I just happened to find the opening and be the first one out. It took all of us to get out."

My three friends smiled knowingly, probably remembering our last Bulldogger adventure when taking too much of the credit after we caught a record catfish in Quicksand Pond made me persona non grata for quite a spell. I could see they were glad I seemed to have truly learned my lesson.

"Well, you boys make a great team. Now, it's time for us to do our thing," Colton said. "I'm sure my brother is eager to see the light of day."

With that, Colton and Jon picked up the harnesses, and Cash, Bo, and Opie carried the chains. BLT and I led Kenworth and Checkers behind them.

"Wow!" Colton said upon reaching the cave. "That is one mighty big tree. Bring your horses over here, and turn them to face away from the entrance."

We did as instructed. Jon and Colton each took a harness collar and placed it over the neck of a horse, before strapping a girth around Kenworth's and Checkers' bellies. Other straps went around the horses' rear ends, and then still other straps attached to those straps. All in all, just getting the horses ready was quite a process.

"You guys still out there," Zane hollered.

"You bet," Colton said. "We don't plan on leaving until you can leave with us. We're outfitting the horses, so they can haul what's left of this tree out of here. Just bear with us a little longer."

Colton turned back to us. "Need you to bring those chains over here," he said. "We're going to wrap them around one end of the tree and then hook them to the harnesses."

I stroked Checkers' neck. "Good boy," I said, softly. "I can't believe we found you! I'm so glad you're okay." Checkers nuzzled my ear.

"Okay, Dru and BLT," Colton said. "Back those horses up some."

We slowly backed the horses until he waved at us to stop. Then Jon and Colton attached the heavy chains to the horse harnesses.

"Okay, guys," Colton said. "I'm going to take it from here."

He attached a long lead line to the bridle on each horse and then stood off to the side. "Your horses are not trained to do heavy labor," he said. "Normally, Percherons or other big work horses are used to move heavy logs and things like this tree. But these horses understand certain commands, so they should be able to move this tree trunk far enough for Randall and Zane to squeeze out of there."

"Checkers has pulled a hay wagon before," I said.

"So has Kenworth," BLT said.

"Well let's hope they remember that," said Colton.

I heard a commotion behind us. BLT must have heard it, too, because we both turned around to look at the same time. Coming down the path was a string of people I had never seen before. The only person who didn't seem surprised to see them was Colton. He just waved.

"Howdy, folks," he said. "I appreciate your coming to help, but please stand back till we get this tree moved." He looked at us. "That means you kids, too."

Colton nodded at the tree. "The way this tree is wedged in the entrance hole, I'm not sure what will happen once we start moving it. And as fine as I am sure your horses are, I also don't know how they are going to respond once the tree starts moving. So let's give them a little space."

"Yes, sir," we all said, and did as we were told.

"Okay, Checkers, Kenny, ah-yah! Get up there now."

The horses lunged forward, bumped into each other, strained against the chains. The tree barely budged. "Get up there," Colton said. "Ah-yah!" He flipped the reins up and down. "Ah-yah!" Again, the horses threw their weight into the collars, and pulled with all their might. The tree groaned and creaked. "Ah-yah! Get up!" More loud creaking and something popped. Bits of wood flew in the air. A tree limb broke and fell with a thump to the ground. Jon hurried over and pulled it out of the way.

"Get up!" Colton said. "Ah-yah!" Checkers and Kenny leaned into their collars again. The chains jangled and clanked. "Get up!"

The tree shivered and shuddered. And then after a lot of cracking and creaking the tree began to move. Checkers and Kenny seemed to sense it was giving and threw their weight into the task, once again. The tree slid a few more feet. The horses took huge steps now, dragging the giant tree trunk farther and farther away from the cave. Colton yelled, "Whoa! Whoa!"

Zane's head appeared in the opening, and he waved. Everyone cheered and clapped. Checkers and Kenny nodded their heads, too, as if taking a bow.

Bo was the first one to reach Zane. He jumped into his father's arms and they hugged like it'd been years not hours since they last saw each other. Colton handed the reins over to someone, and then he and Jon ducked inside the cave. Pretty soon, they came back out carrying Randall in an arm chair, just as we boys had done after the wreck. Colton and Jon stopped by us Bulldoggers. Randall stood, balanced between them.

"I would like to meet your daughter, Jon," Randall said. "My brother has always sung her praises, but now I'd also like to thank her for finding the boys."

BLT stepped forward. "I'm BLT," she said.

"Nice to meet you," Randall said. "We sure appreciate all of your help."

"It was no trouble at all," she said.

147

"I was wondering how you knew to come looking for us in the first place. Did my wife call you?" Randall asked.

"Yes," BLT said. "The way I understand it, when you all didn't show up with the livestock in Pueblo, someone from the junior rodeo tried to reach your cell phone with no luck. He then called your wife, who said she had last talked to you while you were stopped in Guymon for lunch."

"We knew," Jon said, "since you'd picked up the stock after that, you had to be somewhere between Fender ranch and Pueblo."

"No small area to search," Randall said.

"You're right about that. We didn't know whether to look for you on the highway or the back roads either. And then the tornado came through," Colton said, "and all the first responders were out dealing with other emergencies. The twister touched down and spent some time here, so there was a lot to deal with. That slowed down our search."

"Thank you for not giving up," Randall said.

"The biggest clue was when we found your dually upside down in the wash out on that back road," Colton said.

"Honestly, I didn't hold out much hope for you," Jon said. "But when I got closer and realized no one was in the vehicle or trailer, not even the livestock, I felt sure we would find you."

"If I hadn't seen Opie's lucky bandanna," BLT said, "I probably would have gone looking somewhere else."

"I was frantic when that went missing," Opie said, "but it turned out to be a lucky thing I lost it."

"Listen, boys," Colton said. "I'm going to take Randall and Zane over to Boise City to have them looked over by a doctor, but I want you to know all these people have come to help with whatever needs to be done or whatever you need.

"I know you are anxious to get home, and I promise we'll get you there as quickly as possible. In the meantime, Jon and these good folks have seen to it that you will be fed and have a chance to get cleaned up. We shouldn't be gone too long."

"That's mighty nice of you all," I said. The other Bulldoggers nodded agreement.

One of the other men came over and took over for Jon with the horses. Colton and Jon then carried Randall up the path to Colton's truck, but not before Zane had his minute with us. "I am so darn proud of you boys," he said.

We all took turns giving him a hug.

"Bo," Zane said, "I know you want to go with me to the doctor, but I think it would be better for you to stay put and get cleaned up. It sounds like they are putting on a spread for you all—and I know you must be hungry."

"Well, when you put it that way," Bo said, rubbing his belly.

Zane laughed. "That's the son I know. Now I'll be back in two shakes of a squirrel's tail."

He gave Bo's shoulder a hard squeeze, and then turned up the gravel trail.

Jon said, "Boys, I have people here who are going to gather all of your gear and so forth. You have stuff in the cave. Anywhere else?"

"At our campsite," I said, "but BLT said it was all pretty much blown away by the tornado."

"And we have the calves," Bo said.

"I have that covered," Jon said. "There are folks rounding them up as we speak. The stock trailer is fine—even if that brand new truck was totaled. I'm still scratching my head over how lucky you all were. I've been instructed to deliver you to Colton's house. His wife, Yvonne, and my wife,

Vanessa, along with the ladies from the church, have put together a meal for you."

"Thank you, sir," I said. "That sounds great!"

"Sure does," the other Bulldoggers chimed in. "Thanks!"

BLT, who had been standing nearby listening, said, "Since Checkers seems okay with trailing me, I'll ride Kenworth home, and I bet Checkers will follow."

"Works for me," I said. I gave Checkers one more hug and a whispered promise that I'd see him soon, and then I left him in BLT's capable hands.

Jon led the way to his truck and we climbed in. I knew we had to smell like drovers at the end of a long cattle drive, but Jon never even wrinkled his nose, much less commented. As we headed up the long, winding driveway to Colton's, two women came out to greet us.

"Boys," the taller one said. "Come on inside. We have food cooking." I think she was Colton's wife, Yvonne.

We entered through the back door, straight into the kitchen. I took a long whiff of whatever was cooking and nearly passed out from the wonderful aromas.

"I think you have time to shower. Folks have brought an assortment of blue jeans and shirts and underclothes for you to pick from." Yvonne put her hand up beside her mouth as if she were telling us a secret and whispered, "Those underclothes are all new, by the way, still in the package."

We followed her through the kitchen and down a hallway into a bedroom. True to her word, on the bed, an assortment of clothing had been laid out in neat little piles.

With Yvonne's help, we each took a turn choosing something to wear. She held up shirts and jeans, guessing our sizes as best she could.

With our arms filled with garments she led us further

down the hallway and split us up, two to a bathroom. "Towels are in the linen closet, just inside the door on your right," she said.

Bo and I went in the hall bathroom, while Opie and Cash disappeared into a bedroom, which I assumed had its own bath. By the time Bo and I had showered and dressed, Cash and Opie were already in the kitchen. BLT had arrived at the house while we were cleaning up.

Yvonne handed each of us a plate and showed us to where the food had been laid out on the breakfast bar. We filled our plates with brisket, baked beans, potato salad, and deviled eggs. Squares of corn bread and soft butter waited for us at the end of the line. A homemade chocolate cake sat on a pedestal, nearby.

Hardly a word was said as we emptied our plates and filled our bellies. Vanessa walked around the table refilling our glasses with iced tea or lemonade; there was plenty of ice-cold water, too. I must have had five glasses of water before I felt like I had taken the edge off my thirst. I noticed the other Bulldoggers were just as thirsty. If nothing else, we had all gained a new appreciation for the importance of hydration from our adventure.

When we had made some space on our plates, Vanessa brought around trays of more corn bread and deviled eggs, and we piled up again, unable to resist second helpings.

"There's plenty more where that came from," Yvonne said. "Don't be shy."

When I went back for thirds, the rest of the Bulldoggers did, too. Over dessert, we each got a chance to tell our stories from the trip, and hear about what damage the storm had done elsewhere in the county.

We had put a big dent in the chocolate cake by the time I

heard a truck pull in the driveway. Pretty soon Colton, Randall, and Zane walked in the back door, only Randall was in a walking cast now and I could see his shoulder was wrapped. "Something smells awful good," Randall said.

Zane smiled and nodded. "Yes, indeed. Smells like home cooking."

The three men filled their plates twice before all was said and done. They were starting on dessert when we again heard the crunch of gravel, followed by a knock on the door.

Colton opened it wide and said, "Pastor, what a pleasant surprise! Come on in!"

"Surprise, my foot," he said.

"Okay, okay," Colton said, with a sheepish laugh.

"The good pastor here has offered to let us use the church van to transport you all back to Bootleg. Jon usually drives the van on Sundays, bringing folks to church, so he's going to drive you boys. Meanwhile, I'm going to drive the stock home, along with Randall, so he can stretch out on the second seat, and Zane, to keep me company on the drive."

"Yay!" We cheered.

"I never thought I would be so happy to be going back to Bootleg," I said.

We helped take our dishes to the kitchen, but Yvonne and Vanessa waved off our offer to help wash, dry, and put them up. Instead they gave each of us a big hug and a kiss and then turned us back over to the pastor. Jon insisted BLT ride along with us on the return trip so that he would also have company on the long ride back to the Panhandle.

We piled into the church van loaded down with pillows and blankets from the church women's guild.

"I'm too excited to sleep," Cash said. "Why don't we play a game?"

"What kind of game?" BLT asked.

"A road-trip game, of course," Cash said.

"I like how you think, Cash," Bo said, with a grin. "No DVD player required here."

Cash smiled.

"Why don't we count road kill this time instead of yellow vehicles," Opie suggested.

"Well, now that's kind of gross," I said.

"Not really," BLT said. "If you think about it, road kill is just food for another creature."

"Wellll, I guesss," I said, not completely convinced.

"You've all seen turkey vultures, right?" BLT said. "Well my grandmother—she's Kiowa—calls them 'Peace Eagles' because actually they never kill anything. Their beaks are not shaped to even break through the skin of an animal. They're a very misunderstood bird!"

"Wow, I didn't know that," I said. "I thought they were, well, vultures—always hanging around as trouble went down . . . trouble that always seemed to end with something dead in the road surrounded by vultures."

"I know what you mean," BLT said. "When I was young and saw them circling, I always thought it meant they were going in for the kill."

"That's what I always thought, too," Opie said. I liked the fact that Opie didn't seem to mind us knowing that he didn't know everything.

"Nope," BLT said. "Vultures circle like that because the kill is too fresh, and they need to wait a few days while the skin starts to deteriorate. And other times if you see them circling they could simply be riding an updraft. Their wings have a large surface area, so while it is difficult for them to get off the ground it is easy for them to stay in the air."

"I'll never look at vultures circling quite the same," Bo said.

"Then you'll love this," BLT said. "Did you know their wings are silver tipped, so while they're riding those updrafts, they're flashing those silver edges. That attracts other vultures, and they come and ride the updraft, too."

"So, while it might look like they are circling to come in for a kill," Opie said, "in reality, they are just having a float trip with their buds."

"Exactly!" BLT said.

"What did you say your grandmother calls them again," Bo asked.

"Peace Eagles," BLT said. "She told me some shamans wear a vulture feather in their hats because they are called upon to dig into death and disease and they want to be sure they come out unharmed, just like a vulture."

"That is awesome," Bo said.

I coughed. Everybody turned and looked at me.

"Getting back to the game," I said, with a grin. "I think we should assign points according to the *type* of road kill."

"What do you think we might see?" Cash said.

"I have a notepad and pen in the glove box, if you need one," Jon said. BLT dug them out. "Ready," she said.

"I'll start you off," Jon said. "It's not unusual to see skunks and armadillos on the road—they're plentiful out here."

"Deer," Bo said. "Red-tailed hawks. Possums."

"Coyotes," BLT said.

"Turtles and raccoons and horny toads," Bo said.

"Rattlesnakes and tarantulas," I said.

"Bobcats," Jon said. "And mountain lions, on occasion."

"I had no idea Oklahoma had so much wildlife!" Cash said.

"I think," I said, "the animals should be worth more points if we see them alive."

"Absolutely," Opie said. "It's more exciting to see a live wild animal, and it's a more rare event."

That settled, we figured out a point system and then glued our eyes on the windows as we rode along.

"You guys," BLT said, "are a lot of fun on a road trip."

"Now that I'm a reformed whiner," Cash said. All the Bulldoggers hooted at that. BLT looked a bit confused.

"It's true," Cash told her. "I'll tell you all about it someday."

"I noticed this van has a DVD player, Cash," I said.

"Saw that," he said. "But I think it's more fun watching for live critters along the road."

Eventually the sun went down, and the night slipped into its place, until we could no longer see out the windows. We pulled out pillows and blankets and got a little shut-eye.

* * * * * *

Next thing I knew, Jon was saying, "Boys, you're home!"

I opened my eyes and looked out the van window. We were at Scotty's house, and all of the families—my mom and dad (and my little brother, Kevin); Mr. and Mrs. Bennett; Mr. George; and even Cecil and his grandmother—had come to welcome us home.

As Jon pulled in and stopped, I realized that even though we had never made it to Colorado, or gotten to see Pikes Peak for that matter, I didn't really care. I was happy to be home, safe and sound.

Chapter 29
Home, at Last

ONE WEEK AFTER our big road trip to the Oklahoma Panhandle, I called a meeting of the Bulldoggers Club at Scotty's house. My mother had made an extra pot of chicken and noodles and wanted me to deliver it for her, so it seemed logical to meet there.

According to the Bulldoggers' grapevine, Randall had had to have surgery on his ankle after the bone started healing funny. I figured most of that was probably true, but I still wanted to hear the details straight from the horse's mouth, as folks like to say.

After we arrived, Randall called everyone into their family room, where he was propped up in his recliner. The stark white cast on his leg threw me off at first. It looked awful serious. But I couldn't help also notice that he and Scotty looked like a matched set of book ends what with Scotty's arm being in a cast, too. Scotty was sitting in the overstuffed chair, his arm resting on a pillow in his lap. "Good to see you all home safe and sound," Scotty said.

"Yeah, what a crazy couple of days," I said. "Sorry to have brought your dad back in worse shape than we left you!"

"We sure could have used you on the trip!" Bo added.

That made Scotty smile.

"Have a seat, boys," Randall said. "Zane should be here soon. He had a little errand to run."

Cash and Opie plopped down on the long, green corduroy sofa. Bo chose the ottoman in front of Scotty's chair. I sat cross-legged on the braided rug and leaned back against the love seat, opposite Randall's recliner.

Before Randall could continue, Arlene came in with a tray of homemade oatmeal cookies and glasses and a pitcher of lemonade. She poured each of us a glass. The cookies were just the way I like them, with melted chocolate chips and pecan halves on top.

"Thank you, ma'am," each of us said, as she passed the plate of cookies.

"Thank your mother, Dru, for the thoughtful gift. I know everyone will enjoy the chicken and noodles. She makes the best recipe in the county."

"That's quite the compliment, coming from you, Mrs. Fender. I'll be sure to tell her you said that," I said. "And we'd all like to say thank you for the ice chest of food and snacks—it sure came in handy on the trip."

"Well you boys are welcome," she said. "I'm just glad you're all home in one piece."

Once she had returned to the kitchen, Randall said, "Zane and I have a few things to cover with you, so we'll just wait till he gets here."

"Yes, sir," we all chimed, our mouths full of cookies.

While we wait for Zane, we played catch up with Scotty, and shortly thereafter, Zane came in carrying a brown paper sack under his arm. He sat on the end of the sofa closest to Randall. He gave Randall a nod, and Randall started the meeting.

"Now that we're safely home, I want to let you boys know that we were lucky out there. Things could have played out very differently. There was never a guarantee that we would get a happy ending on this trip," Randall said.

"I also know you've been worried about how our no-show impacted the Pueblo rodeo. Well, I am happy to say when the organizers heard on the news how bad the storm was, they implemented their backup contingency plan. Except for being a little soggy—Pueblo got rain, too—the rodeo went off without a hitch." We all cheered at that news.

"I know you're also disappointed about missing the rodeo and seeing Colorado, but I can promise you that we'll make that up to you. You have plenty of road trips and rodeos in your future. What we want to do tonight, however, is commend you boys for your team work and your resourcefulness in the face of so many challenges on this particular trip."

"We are proud," Zane said, "of the compassion and humility you displayed. I know before this trip you didn't know about Opie's encounter with the lawn mower. We are proud of how you boys took that in stride—no pun intended, and that Opie had the courage to share that with you. Sometimes folks have a hard time accepting other's differences. And other times they are too proud to ask for help or admit they aren't perfect."

I raised my hand to speak.

"Go ahead, Dru," Randall said.

"I just wanted to tell Opie that I owe him an apology." I

turned to face Opie. "You may be the calmest kid I know. I don't know how you did it, man. But when things blew up, you kept your head about you and you knew what to do. I'm sorry I wasn't more open to listening to your ideas before."

"It's okay," Opie said. "I know my rambling on and on can be annoying. I just can't help myself sometimes."

"Not one of us is perfect," I said. "I can be short-tempered. And I think Cash wouldn't mind me saying that until very recently he's been known on occasion to whine."

Bo, Scotty, Cecil, and Cash all whooped at that and nodded agreement (Cash nodded the hardest of the lot).

"Thanks Opie for everything you did for us," I said. "I'm proud to have you as a fellow Bulldogger."

Opie pushed his wire-frames higher on his nose. His cheeks glowed red with embarrassment, but it was the good kind of embarrassed.

"Thanks, Dru," Opie said. "I'd also like to thank Cash for helping when he was feeling so poorly. If he hadn't pitched in to get the water jugs onto Checkers' back, I could not have done it alone. And remember, he was the one who found Bo's bandanna full of piñon nuts on the ground. I hate to think how hungry we would have been without those."

"If you recall," Randall said, "Cash was also the one who helped Bo set up the makeshift corral and tied up the tarp for shade." We gave Cash a round of applause.

Randall continued, "I also have some news. I know you boys remember that after the fall he took at the Bear Creek Cove rodeo, Zane was laid up for quite a while. Well, I'm pleased to announce he has accepted my offer to be my new partner and ranch manager."

Another round of applause filled the room.

"I don't know anyone who knows more about livestock

and ranching than Zane. Having him run the ranch will free me up to not only focus more on improving the guest ranch side of the operation but also to spend more time with Arlene and Scotty."

Zane jumped in then. "Enough about us," he said. "Tonight is about you boys. We feel you Bulldoggers behaved mighty heroic in the face of disaster. You have also proven how serious you are about rodeo. We are pleased to tell you, as our way of saying thank you, that you now have a new place to practice."

"Where?" Bo asked, but we were all eager to know.

"Remember the old Circle B Arena? The one down at the end of town?"

"Yes, yes," I said.

"Well we have gotten permission to rename it The Bulldoggers Club Arena. As long as you help to maintain it, that indoor arena is yours to practice in."

We whooped and hollered at that news.

"And," Zane said, once we had quieted down, "I have here a framed copy," he pulled a wood frame from the brown paper sack, "of the old Cowboy Code for you to hang up on the wall in the entry way to the arena. Its based on what were once the unwritten rules of the Old West. I thought given our experience in No Man's Land that you boys would appreciate it. It belonged to my grandpa, who, you might recall, worked alongside the great Bill Pickett, roping cattle. I have to give my grandpa most of the credit for anything I know about horses or ranching, because he taught me everything I know. And I've always tried to live by this code."

Zane passed around the Cowboy Code, and we each took turns admiring it.

"We'll try to live up to this, too, Mr. Gillock," I said.

"I know you will," Zane said.

Zane continued. "You boys might also like to know that BLT and her family will be moving soon to Bootleg."

"That's great," I said, "but what brings them here?"

"BLT's mother is from Bootleg, and her grandmother is getting on in years and needs someone to take care of her. We have an opening on the ranch here, so BLT's father has asked if he could transfer," Randall said. "I expect you boys to make her feel welcome."

"We'll be happy to do that," I said. "We had wanted to do something anyway to thank her for rescuing us."

All the other Bulldoggers nodded.

"And one more thing," Randall said. "Remember those giant bones Bo discovered in the arroyo?"

We all nodded. I noticed Bo was suddenly very attentive.

"Well, I had a paleontologist—a scientist who studies dinosaur bones—check them out. They are definitely dinosaur bones. She's not sure just yet, but she thinks you might have discovered a whole new dinosaur no one has ever seen before, at least in these parts."

"And, get this," Randall said. "Turns out she knew all about that map the Man with Two Names was carrying. She says it was not a treasure map, but rather a fossil hunter's map from around the 1850s. The Man with Two Names wasn't hunting buried treasure; he was looking for fossils. The map must have been stolen during one of William Coe's looting parties, and he simply held onto it."

Zane said, "I know Randall said the credit for the find should go to Bo, and I agree with that. However, I'd also like to think finds like that belong to all of us, to all Americans, especially to the scientists who study fossils and share their knowledge so we can all better understand this world we live in. I've talked it over with Bo, and he agrees. Bo, you want to tell them?"

"I've decided to donate the bones to the Natural History Museum at the University of Oklahoma in Norman," Bo said. "If that's okay with you, Mr. Fender."

"I think that's a generous idea befitting a true Bulldogger," Randall said.

"The museum plans to set up a scholarship fund in Bo's name at the university," Zane added. "That way students who want to become paleontologists but can't afford to attend college will have funds to help them pay for tuition as well as their room and board and books."

"That's awesome," I said.

"Way to go, Bo," Opie said, and started clapping.

Everyone joined in until Bo was blushing redder than his long underwear. As the applause faded, I stood up.

"Yes, Dru," Randall said.

"Sir, I don't know about the heroic part, but I do know we Bulldoggers are changed in ways that are hard to put into words. None of us will ever forget our first road trip through No Man's Land."

"Hear! Hear!"

The real buried treasure of friendship and knowledge had turned out to be far more valuable and longer lasting than a chest full of stolen gold and silver coins. Seems that was what the Man with Two Names had been trying to tell us all along.

Maybe now he could rest in peace.

Bulldogger Lingo
(and other terms)

arroyo: a steep-sided gully cut by running water

bareback: to ride a horse without a saddle

Bill Pickett: an African-American-Cherokee cowboy from Texas, recognized by two halls of fame as the sole inventor of bulldogging, or steer wrestling, the only rodeo event that can be attributed to a single individual; his unique method of bulldogging steers involved jumping from his horse to a steer's back, biting the steer's upper lip (no longer allowed), and throwing the steer to the ground by its horns

bison: any of several large shaggy-maned mammals having a large head with short horns and heavy forequarters, also known in North America as buffalo

bridle: a device that fits on a horse's head used for guiding and controlling the horse, i.e. headgear consisting of buckled straps to which a bit and reins are attached

buffalo wallow: shallow undrained depression on the Great Plains, often containing water in wet seasons, and generally thought to have been produced or deepened by the rolling and wallowing of herds of buffalo in mud and dust

bulldogger: also steer wrestler; one who wrestles steers

bulldogging: also steer wrestling; a rodeo event in which a cowboy jumps from his horse, grabs a steer by the horns, and flips it over onto the ground while being timed

catch-rope: a rope used to lasso steers and whatnot

cattle guard: a metal grid covering a ditch, allowing vehicles and pedestrians to pass over but not cattle

cattle rustler: one who steals cattle

dead zone: a place where unable to receive a mobile phone or radio signal

dually: pickup truck with four wheels on its rear axle

escarpment: long, steep slope separating two flat areas

fraidy hole: an underground storm shelter; used to avoid being sucked up by a tornado and flung to Kingdom Come

Great Plains: a vast prairie region extending from Alberta, Saskatchewan, and Manitoba in Canada south through the west central United States into Texas

halter: straps that buckle around a horse's head to facilitate tying and leading

lead rope: a rope with a snap on one end that can be attached to the halter and used to lead and tie horses

mesa: a hill that has a flat top and steep sides

No Man's Land: a narrow strip of land thirty-four miles wide between Kansas and Texas extending from the 100th parallel on the east to the 103rd parallel on the west, 168 miles in length; eventually it became the Oklahoma Panhandle

Oklahoma Panhandle: the extreme western region of the state of Oklahoma, comprising Cimarron, Texas, and Beaver counties; its name comes from its shape, which recalls the handle on a cooking pan

pickup: a small truck with an enclosed cab and open back

piñon nuts: edible seed of small pine tree native to Mexico and the southwestern United States

prickly pear: a cactus with jointed stems and oval flattened segments, having barbed bristles and large pear-shaped, prickly fruits

shortgrass prairie: ecosystem of North American Great Plains, extending from eastern foothills of Rocky Mountains to Nebraska, north into Saskatchewan, and south into the high plains of Colorado, Oklahoma, Texas, New Mexico

solar still: a simple way of distilling water, using the heat of the sun, to create water cleaner than the purest rainwater

stock: also livestock, domestic animals, raised for home use or profit, especially on a farm or ranch

steer wrestler: also bulldoggers; one who wrestles steers

steer wrestling: also bulldogging; a rodeo event in which a cowboy jumps from his horse, grabs a steer by the horns, and flips it over onto the ground while being timed

stock trailer: a trailer that transports livestock

storm cellar: also known as a fraidy hole; an underground shelter used to avoid being sucked up by a tornado and flung to Kingdom Come

tornado: a violently rotating column of air, which, to be considered a tornado, must be in contact with both the ground and the cloud base

tack: equipment used in horseback riding, including the saddle and bridle

tack room: a room, often in a barn or out building, for storing saddles and other gear for horseback riding, including saddle blankets, ropes, chaps, bridles, and bits

wallow: to roll about in mud or water; a depression in the ground where mammals go to wallow

Mrs. Winterhalter's
Chicken and Noodles

4 pounds fryer chicken pieces
1 tablespoon salt
2 bay leaves
1 eight-ounce package sliced mushrooms
1 sixteen-ounce bag frozen crinkle-cut carrots
1 fourteen-ounce bag frozen peas
1 rib of celery plus leaves, diced
2 teaspoons chopped fresh thyme
1 teaspoon dill weed
  Pepper to taste
1 sixteen-ounce package large homemade egg noodles
1/2 cup flour
1/2 cup water

Fill a large pot with water. Add the chicken and a tablespoon of salt and the bay leaves. Bring the water to a boil. Reduce heat and simmer for one hour. Remove the chicken from the pot and place on a platter. Debone the chicken and add the meat back to the water. Add the vegetables and seasonings. Cover the pot with a lid and simmer for one hour. Remove the bay leaves. Add in the noodles and bring to a boil, again.

In a two-cup liquid measuring cup, add the flour. Mix in the 1/2 cup of water until smooth. Slowly pour the mixture into the pot with the chicken, vegetables, and noodles, stirring constantly. Continue stirring until it comes to a boil again. Keep stirring as it thickens. Allow it to boil for five more minutes.

Tip: Save enough of the chicken and noodles for a few meals, and then divide the rest into smaller servings and freeze for lunches.

Yield: Eight to ten servings.

Acknowledgments

Many thanks to all those who helped bring this story to the page:

Much appreciation goes to Debby Kinnard, historical interpreter, who gave me an informative and lengthy tour of Alabaster Caverns in Freedom, Oklahoma, one beautiful January day.

A big thank you to John Loy of Green Country Truck Sales, Tulsa, Oklahoma, for generously providing information about stock trailers and directing me to a manufacturer in Iowa. Many thanks go to Nicole Ausdemore-Watts and the engineering department at Featherlite Trailers, Cresco, Iowa, for e-mailing photographs of the trailers and for verification.

Tom Wolf, fisheries biologist, lifetime friend, and perpetual Boy Scout, thank you for loaning me a rare book about native Oklahoma grasses and plants and for always being prepared to help in any way I need. Game Warden Max Crocker of Guymon County, thank you for answering my many questions and for setting me straight on black-tailed jackrabbits.

A word of gratitude to the Oklahoma Historical Society, publishers of *The Encyclopedia of Oklahoma History* (what would writers do without such wonderful reference works), and the Will Rogers Memorial in Claremore, Oklahoma, for keeping the wise words of Oklahoma's favorite son both preserved and available to a new generation.

Thanks also to the website www.LegendsofAmerica.com/ok-williamcoe.html, for providing information about the infamous William Coe.

Clarence Wells, former dog groomer for my gentlemanly Scottish terrier, thoroughbred horse expert, builder of anything and everything one could imagine: Thank you for answering my calls every time because you know I am on deadline and need to know now! You are a good friend! I am lucky to have you on my side.

Beverly Frasier, dear friend and cracker of whips, thank you for handling innumerable tasks and taking very good care of the things I hold most dear to my heart—my sweet teenage daughter and my two doggies, so that I might continue to do the work that I love.

Much love and many kisses and hugs to my two daughters (and Bev, too) who listened to me read this story, several times, and who offered good suggestions every single time.

Michael Dylan Welch, haiku master, and exacting copy-editor, thank you for joining us on this adventure.

Jeanne Devlin, editor extraordinaire, thanks for being patient with me and always starting off every conversation—editorial or otherwise—with a positive comment.

About the Author

Barbara Hay is author of the award-winning juvenile series the Bulldoggers Club as well as the acclaimed young adult novel, *Lesson of the White Eagle*. *The Bulldoggers Club—The Tale of the Ill-Gotten Catfish*, the first book in the Bulldoggers Club series, was published in 2012. A widowed mother of four children, she lives and writes at her home in Oklahoma. Visit her at www.BarbaraHay.com.